Now to the Stars

Captain W. E. Johns was born in 1893. After active service in the army, he joined the RFC in 1916 and flew bombers in France until 1918 when he was shot down, wounded and captured. After the First World War he stayed on in the RAF for some years before leaving to try his hand at journalism. He began writing stories for magazines as well and was so successful that he became a full time author. A very imaginative writer, he produced hundreds of adventure stories for children. His most famous character is 'Biggles', whose exploits fill nearly a hundred books.

Captain Johns lived for several years in Scotland – the Earth 'setting' for his space adventures – but later moved to a house at Hampton Court, where he died in 1968.

Captain W. E. Johns

Now to the Stars

An Interplanetary Adventure

Piccolo Books

First published 1956 by Hodder and Stoughton Ltd
This Piccolo edition published 1980 by Pan Books Ltd,
Cavaye Place, London SW10 9PG
© W. E. Johns (Publications) Ltd 1956
ISBN 0 330 26033 2
Made and printed in Great Britain by
C. Nicholls & Company Ltd, Philips Park Press, Manchester

Contents

1 Prelude to adventure   7

2 Borron tells some tales   16

3 To Mino and beyond   24

4 The unlucky land of Lin   35

5 Worlds of Wonder   46

6 The peculiar people of Norro   56

7 The little beasts of Kund   67

8 The Terror   75

9 World without a name   84

10 Strange sanctuary   91

11 Stars in their courses   102

12 A tragedy of the past   113

13 All or none   123

14 Out of the frying-pan ...   132

15 The man eater of Mars   142

16 The final problem   151

1 Prelude to adventure

A scientist once remarked that with so many people in the world there would always, at any moment, be two doing the same thing and thinking the same thought.

Rex Clinton, sitting on a kitbag in the moonlight, surrounded by a sea of heather in the remote Highlands of Scotland, would have disputed this. He would have declared that no one was doing what he was doing, or sharing his thoughts; and in this conviction he would have been justified, for what he was actually doing was waiting for a spacecraft to take him to Mars: and as for his thoughts, his mind was running on the people he knew on that planet – and, indeed, on the planetoids beyond.

It is true that these worlds and the people on them were known to a few other people; Group-Captain 'Tiger' Clinton, his father; Doctor 'Toby' Paul, his father's friend; and Professor Lucius Brane, whose 'cosmobile' (as he called it) the *Spacemaster*, had made their interplanetary flights possible. But they were busy checking the materials and equipment that had been promised to certain people who were engaged in the formidable task of making Mars once more habitable after the overwhelming disaster that had swept away almost every form of life, human, animal and vegetable.

Let it not be supposed that Rex's thoughts were entirely cheerful. In a way he was looking forward to the coming voyage, and would not have been left behind; yet he was also aware of the heart-shrinking fear that would grip him when he saw Earth, with all the things he knew and understood,

7

diminish to a flickering spark of light before fading altogether in the awful empty spaces of the Universe.

He was older than when he had made his first voyage to the Moon, not only in age but in outlook. He felt that he had lost something – something to do with the emotion of wonder, or surprise. Nothing could really be wonderful any more because, as he perceived, nothing was impossible. That word could be used only in a local sense. On Earth a butterfly with a wing spread of ten feet was impossible simply because such insects did not occur on Earth, although elsewhere that might be the normal size. On Mars a whale would be held equally impossible, because there were no whales. Once one accepted that, he reflected, then nothing was impossible. Conversely, anything, however fantastic, became possible.

Rex wondered what impossibilities they would encounter on their coming voyage. Even on Earth, he pondered, as men discovered new lands they found new creatures, some of which strained the credulity – flying fish and fish that climbed trees, for example. If such discoveries could be made on Earth, what might be expected from other worlds?

Such thoughts as these, and the knowledge he had acquired, had not only changed his whole outlook on life but in some curious way seemed to have isolated him from those people who still believed that in all the Universe there was but one world – their own.

There were times when he wished he could share their ignorance and think of the world as he had when a small boy; a beautiful place of land and water, of hills and valleys, of trees and flowers, with its own sun and moon and stars destined to float for ever in a sky serenely blue. Now he knew that this was not so, although, to be sure, Earth was still the most perfect of all the worlds he had seen. But he knew that it was only one of a million heavenly bodies rolling round their eternal orbits where such words as time and weight and distance were meaningless; where, by a whim of that incomprehensible force called gravity, a world could disappear in a flash, as utterly as a pinch of gunpowder cast into a furnace.

The thought that the Earth he loved, and everything on it, all the work that men had ever done, might vanish as if it had never existed, depressed him terribly; and for that reason it angered him that a few men, having in their curiosity discovered how to break the atoms of which all matter is composed, should risk annihilation, not only of themselves but of others. This was what they called the March of Progress, and apparently nothing could stop it.

His eyes turned from the sombre landscape to the star-studded dome of heaven. Disillusionment, he felt, was his punishment for curiosity, as it so often is. No longer was that friendly disc, the Moon, a beacon put there to shed a gentle radiance after night had taken possession of the land. He knew it for what it really was; a mass of meteor-blasted rock and sand which, when not a desolation of frozen sterility, was a wilderness flayed by the merciless sun.

Twinkle, twinkle little star! Never again would he wonder what they were. Never again could they be like diamonds in the sky; for he had stood on some of them and knew the unromantic truth – knew that he himself, at that moment, was sitting on just such a star. It seemed a sad thing to shatter the old illusion. Yet there were compensations. Had he not been to Mino he would never have known Morino, the girl who had laughed at his clumsy efforts to fly on her wings.

His eyes wandered to the planet that was to be their destination. It was a pity, he pondered bitterly, that the nuclear experts, so busily engaged in their work of destruction, could not see the fragments of the lost Kraka, torn asunder by a lunatic experiment. Jupiter still smouldered from that same devastating explosion: Saturn, girdled by atomic dust that had yet to settle: Mars, almost stripped of its

9

air, water and vegetation, by the stupendous blast. But then, mused Rex, if the Professor revealed these sobering facts, who would believe him? Very few. Least of all those to whom the warning should be directed. Not even the reporter who had seen them land on their return from Mars, and could therefore tell the most sensational story of all time, had dared to utter a word for fear of being called a madman or a liar. The truth was, Rex supposed, the people of Earth were not yet ready for interstellar flight. A comparatively young civilization, they had barely recovered from the shock of ordinary flight. Well, one day they would have to accept it, whether they liked it or not.

Nevertheless, public opinion had swung from incredulity to questioning suspicion during the past few months. There had been much talk of 'Flying Saucers' and the like. People, not one person but many, had seen objects in the sky for which no acceptable explanation had been forthcoming. Unidentified Flying Objects the newspapers called them. Why should people be so loath to accept the truth? wondered Rex. Radar screens do not lie. They can only reveal what is there. They cannot register an object that is not there.

This sort of publicity had upset the Professor who suspected that the *Spacemaster* was to some extent responsible for it, although his was not the only spacecraft that had visited Earth. He also suspected that his base at Glensalich Castle was being watched, for which reason he had decided against building another ship of his own. Instead, when he was ready to leave Earth on another extra-terrestrial survey flight it would be in the ship captained by Gator Faro, of the Minoan Interstellar Exploration Squadron. Gator had promised to come within sighting distance of Earth at regular intervals to watch for signals. Well, the signal had been set, and the astronauts were waiting for the 'Saucer' to arrive.

Rex hoped the same ship would come; the one that had

brought them home after their own craft, the *Spacemaster*, had collapsed in space as a result of metal fatigue. Rex still shuddered at the memory of that awful shipwreck, in the dreadful silent vacuum, that pitiless void, that occurs between the bodies of the Solar System.

What other ships might have come within Earth's atmosphere he did not know, unless they were units of the Remote Survey Fleet commanded by the ambitious Rolto Mino, who had advocated the conquest of Earth as an alternative to the restoration of Mars, to solve the Minoan overcrowding problem.

Such were Rex's thoughts as he sat on the desolate Scottish moor awaiting the arrival of the craft that would take them and their luggage to Mars, and, if the Professor had his way, beyond. For the Professor's great ambition now was the exploration of the planetoids, a project that might well occupy him for the rest of his life. And that would only be a beginning. Beyond lay worlds without end, the exploration of which would occupy men till the end of time itself.

The preparation of those things which were to help in the restoration of Mars had been the Professor's chief occupation for three months, for, as he averred, the introduction of any form of life into new conditions was an experiment that called for caution. There had been demonstrations of this on Earth, notably in Australia, where the rapid multiplications of the common wild rabbit had become a serious problem. Already one example had occurred on Mars, where a special insecticide, intended to destroy the malignant mosquitoes, had accelerated the growth of all forms of life to an incredible – not to say alarming – degree.

Tools and inanimate objects, such as spacesuits, did not matter. The Minoan suits were better, but were not fitted with radio. And no machinery was included, for the Martians would have none of it, having learned a bitter lesson in the distant past when, in their machine age, the people found they were on their way to becoming the slaves of what were intended to be labour-saving devices. The Professor said he was thinking particularly of seeds, seeds of trees for re-afforestation and vegetables for food. There was a hamper of young ducks, and another of chickens. These, by their eggs, it was hoped, would also help to solve the food problem. Eggs, for a stock of birds, would have been easier to carry, but there might have been some difficulty in hatching them. Whether the birds would live or die, or, if they lived, how they would develop in the novel conditions, was a matter for conjecture. Rather against the Professor's advice Rex was taking Morino a kitten. The whole business, he thought, was reminiscent of Noah's Ark.

His reverie was broken by the arrival of the rest of the party, including Judkins, the Professor's butler-mechanic, who had only come to see them off, for as his services would not be required he was to remain at the castle to deal with inquisitive visitors. Rex reported that he had seen no sign of the spaceship. 'I hope they don't land in the wrong place,' he added anxiously.

'That shouldn't happen,' answered the Professor confidently. 'The green lights are on, as we arranged, and both Gator and Vargo, who will I expect be on board, have seen the place. Vargo came home with us, you remember, for that express purpose. The night is still young.'

'I think they're coming now,' said Tiger. 'A moment ago I saw a star blotted out. As there are no clouds, that could only mean an aircraft of some sort. Whatever it was it isn't showing navigation lights so it can't be an ordinary plane.'

'I can see it – I can see it. Here they come!' exclaimed Rex suddenly, a surge of excitement in his voice.

Presently they could all see it, a black, mushroom-shaped object silhouetted against the pale light of the sky. It grew larger, quickly, silently. The Professor raised an arm, and the beam of a torch cut a wedge of green light in the darkness.

A minute or two later a dark shadow settled with no more noise than a parachute close beside them.

As they hastened towards it the door of the airlock chamber was opened and a tall slim figure stood clear cut against the eerie luminosity of the 'Saucer's' interior.

'Vargo,' called Rex, delightedly.

'Rex,' answered the Martian, in his thin, precise voice. He stepped down, and was soon shaking hands with them to show that he had not forgotten their method of greeting. He was breathing heavily. 'Excuse me,' he said, tapping his chest. 'Your air is strong before I am used to it. My lungs are perhaps too big. Also, here my legs become lead. You are ready to come?'

'Everything is prepared,' replied the Professor briskly.

'Good. Then I will ask Gator to make quick the loading.'

'This is a bigger ship, isn't it?' queried Rex.

'Yes. A new one. Gator has just fetched it from Ando.'

'How are things on Mars?' asked Tiger, as the luggage was stowed.

'Things go well,' stated Vargo. 'When you come things will go better.'

'Have you been to Mino lately?' asked Rex, with affected carelessness.

'Yes, I was there to report progress to the High Council. A friend of yours there was asking if I had been to Earth.'

'Morino?'

'Yes. If I see you I am to say she has a new pair of wings waiting for you.'

'You can talk of these frivolities later,' broke in the Professor. 'Let us get away before some interfering busybody comes along and asks questions. By the way, Vargo, did you find my poor old *Spacemaster* on your way home?'

'Yes, it was still where we left it,' answered Vargo. 'Not that it could be otherwise. We dare not leave it there to be a danger to other ships.'

'You said you would take it in tow and cast it off to fall on Phobos, where it could do no harm,' remindeed Rex.

'True. But Gator thought you might wish to examine it for the cause of the failure, so on second thoughts we took it to Mars, where you will find it.'

'Capital!' exclaimed the Professor. 'I would indeed like to see the state of the metal.'

'The steel in which you put your trust now crumbles in the hand like old wood,' declared Vargo. 'Our orichalcum lasts for ever.'

'What about the mosquitoes?' inquired Rex.

'All that were near our town which you call Utopia, and which we now call Utopia in your honour, have disappeared. We think they grew too big too quickly, and died from not having strength to live. The same with most of the other creatures which lived in the swamps of the old canal, now being reopened by our workmen. The problem is food. We need little, but we must have some, and it must come from Mino or Lentos. With more ships there will be more food, and with more men the work will go faster. But you cannot repopulate a world, that has long been dead, in a single sun cycle. One thing you will be pleased to know for your comfort, there is more air for breathing.'

'More air?' echoed the Professor. 'Where is it coming from?'

'The planet must be collecting some from space,' answered Vargo. 'We, from our travels, knew of places in space where air could be found, always moving slowly towards the nearest orbit. That which was lost from Kraka, and taken from Mars, had to go somewhere. You may have lost some from Earth by your great explosions. On every planet the air becomes

14

more or less. Some is collected. Some is dragged away by comets, passing close. Some, our scientists say, is released from holes which are made in the ground.'

'Very interesting,' murmured the Professor.

By this time the work of loading was complete. Judkins waved goodbye and stepped back. The airlock doors were closed. Rex strapped himself in his seat. The crew took their stations. In the queer unnatural light, with their shining skins and strange luminous eyes, they now looked what they were – men from another world.

The Professor said to Vargo, while pressure was being adjusted: 'Please spare us as much discomfort as possible in the early acceleration. We are in no hurry.'

'It shall be slow,' promised Vargo.

A minute later the ship began to move, and Rex braced himself for the strain that would crush him into his seat as the spacecraft gained escape velocity.

In the event it was not too bad, and in twenty minutes he was able to relax, unconscious of any feeling of movement although he knew they were shooting through the void beyond the Earth's atmosphere at a speed approaching that of those mysterious cosmic rays from which the ship derived its motive power, or as the Martians called it, Energy. Eventually, he thought, the scientists on Earth would capture that same power. They knew about it, and it was in pursuit of it that they had unfortunately found the path that had led to the atom bomb. The exigencies of war had distracted them from their original purpose, and put them on a road which might cause Earth to follow Kraka to oblivion.

He turned his head slowly to the observation window and saw that Earth was already a section of a mighty globe. The part they had left was still in darkness, but across Asia was creeping the dawn of another day.

2 Borron tells some tales

Long before the spaceship – which they learned had been named *Tavona* after a friendly Outer Star – touched down on Mars, Rex could see the scar near Utopia that marked the spot where the canal was being reopened to provide a water supply for the prospective immigrants who, he thought whimsically, would be 'displaced persons' in the widest possible sense. But then, he reflected, given spaceships, the transport of people from world to world was no more trouble than from continent to continent on Earth.

The scar was little more than a straight black line comprising the actual channel and the ground prepared for cultivation on either side of it; but it was conspicuous by reason of the dull uniformity of the rest of the planet. For this, the absence of physical features, mountains, valleys and rivers, was largely responsible. He wondered how long it would be before the scar was spotted by some sharp-eyed astronomer on Earth. The discovery would give the experts something to talk about. They would have to ascribe to it some form of life, for while nature unaided can make marks, and often does, it seldom draws straight lines.

As the ship sank through the thin dry air towards the central landing square, on which two spacecraft were already standing, details became more clearly defined, and Rex was surprised to see how much work had been done. This was explained by the number of upturned faces, both on the square, where the silted dust of ages had disappeared, and on the banks of the canal. The result was an atmosphere of life and activity instead of the death and desolation that had possessed the place on the occasion of their first visit. The jungle still marked the course of the canal towards the Pole, but of the insect hordes there was no sign. All this, pondered Rex in a sort of wonder, was the work of one man. The Professor. But for his genius Mars might have remained a dead world until the end of time. So it seemed that while some men were risking the destruction of one world, another had gone out of his way to save one.

The *Tavona* scraped gently on the paving stones and they were back on Mars. Vargo opened the door, and breathing somewhat faster than usual they stepped down. And the odd thing about it was, thought Rex, the feeling of remoteness of which he had been so conscious during the trip at once disappeared. The reason, he decided, was this: had he not known he was on Mars he might well have supposed that they had merely landed in a foreign country on Earth. Clearly, the day would come when the people on Earth, once they became accustomed to the idea, would think no more of a trans-space flight than a trans-Atlantic one.

He noticed that one of the ships standing near them bore the blue-star insignia of Rolto's Remote Survey Fleet. Indeed, he could see Rolto himself, talking to his crew. He wondered if the man was really to be trusted; if he had really abandoned his project for the conquest of Earth – conquest in this case meaning the vaporization of the entire population.

The day was spent unloading the stores and fixing up one of the many empty houses as a temporary home. Heating, for the cold nights, was a problem, for the Minoans knew nothing of coal and rarely burnt wood, which was precious. For cooking they used the radiant heat of the sun. Vargo got the new arrivals out of the difficulty by giving them a solar ray storage battery, a device that accumulated heat by day and discharged it slowly when required.

The ducks and chickens were released. As the Professor

remarked with a twinkle in his eye, they could hardly fly home. They caused a sensation, for the Minoans had never seen anything like them. The effect, mused Rex, had probably been much the same when the first tropical birds, with their highly coloured plumage, had been introduced into England. The chickens at once started pecking about as if to them one world was as good as another. And when the ducks, seemingly by instinct, made for the canal, they were watched by incredulous eyes. Rex freed his kitten, which made itself at home.

The Professor was soon busy with Vargo, handing over the insecticide and explaining the operation of the spray gun, which was now to be used on the more distant canals where the mosquitoes persisted. This work, it was hoped, could be left to the Minoan crews, for the Professor was anxious to move on to the planetoids.

Later they all walked over to the wreck of the *Spacemaster*, which was standing just outside the town. It was found that the steel outer skin, and the ducts of the power units, had so far deteriorated that they could be broken by hand, either as a result of exposure to different atmospheres or by the bombardment of meteoric dust, or cosmic rays. Some of the equipment inside was found to be serviceable, although for the moment it would not be needed.

As they were near it they went on to examine the freshly dug ground. It appeared to be good healthy loam, and the Professor saw no reason why the seed-planting should not begin forthwith. It could be done by the workmen who had had experience of cultivation on Mino or Lentos. They had, in fact, already planted seeds of their own varieties of grain and vegetables. Some of these resembled closely those of Earth, but others were entirely different, such as the bitter-tasting pods, and the enormous purple roots, which had been found growing near the Pole when the *Spacemaster* had landed there.

Just before sundown, while the Earth party were having tea, another ship arrived with supplies and more men. Vargo brought over the Navigator, whom he said was a man of great experience, having served all his life in the Remote Survey Fleet. He had been to nearly every planetoid at one time or another. His name was Borron, and he was, incidentally, Morino's father – as Vargo informed Rex with a meaning smile.

Rex was on the point of protesting that this meant nothing to him, but remembering in time that Vargo might be reading his mind, he said nothing.

Borron was, of course, exactly the sort of man the Professor was anxious to meet, and with Vargo acting as interpreter he began asking the questions that were uppermost in his mind. Rex poured each visitor a cup of tea. Vargo who had often drunk tea with them, and knew that it had no ill-effect on him, accepted his cup with a smile; but Borron looked at the beverage suspiciously. However, after one or two cautious sips, he, too, smiled.

'Good?' queried Rex.

'Good,' said Vargo.

'Good,' said Borron.

Rex suspected that it was the sweetness that appealed to them, for while there was a sugar content in their root vegetables, cane sugar, so much stronger, was unknown.

Some of the answers given by Borron to the Professor's questions were normal, and might have been anticipated; but others were startling, and somewhat alarming.

Borron stated that while every planet and planetoid was composed of the same basic elements, primary rock, metals and gases, the amount of each was variable. He knew of one composed almost entirely of iron, and another of igneous rock that had fused to something in the nature of glass. Every planetoid, and every Outer Planet, that he had visited, was in some way different according to size, composition and atmosphere; but the fundamental laws of Nature were constant, everywhere. Supreme control was maintained by gravity. It could not, he asserted, be otherwise, or the worlds would always be in collision, with results beyond imagination. Yet no matter what the condition, there was usually some form of life. There was even life on planets where the air was deadly to men. Of what these atmospheres were composed he did not know. Such places were useless, and once they had been recognized as such they were left alone. Exploration without a guide was very dangerous.

This, Rex thought, was pretty obvious. He also perceived, even before the Professor remarked on it, that the big mistake on Earth, in considering the possibility of life on other planets, was the supposition that in order to produce and sustain life the conditions would have to be exactly the same as those on Earth. It might be true that in order to produce the forms of life found on Earth the conditions would have to be much the same, if not identical. But from what Borron said, and he said it in the most matter-of-fact way as if there was nothing surprising about it, it was evident that any set of conditions could produce its own forms of life. That being so, the possibilities defied the wildest conjectures.

This was confirmed when Borron tried to describe some of the things he had seen, things which, in the early days of interplanetary exploration, had caused surprise, but no longer did so. Men, or creatures in the general form of men, were common, although they varied in size from dwarfs to giants. Either way, they were usually the dominant form of life on the planet concerned. Otherwise, where there were no men, the chief form of life might be insects, reptiles or vegetation. Remembering the mosquitoes on Mars Rex could understand this.

Borron went on to say that he knew of one planetoid inhabited by primitive shapeless creatures which, from his description, sounded like dry-land jellyfish. This again was not hard to believe, for if jellyfish could occur in water on Earth, why not on land elsewhere? As far as men were concerned, continued Borron, he thought their degree of intelligence depended on the time the particular world had been in existence, and how long the type of man had had for development. There was another world, a fairly large one, too, alleged Borron in a tone of deep disgust, where the people were so short of food that they were now eating each other, the victims being selected by a special committee.

Rex, remembering that cannibalism had persisted on Earth to the present day, saw nothing particularly remarkable in this, either. But to Borron it was evidently a rare vice.

There was yet another planetoid, a dreadful place, on which war between the tribes had raged for so long that certain flesh-eating animals, to which dead warriors had been cast for disposal, had now so got the upper hand that the surviving human population, faced with extermination, had to live in holes in the ground, only venturing out in numbers. Where these people had come from in the first place nobody knew. They were not of Martian extraction.

'That, some people think, is why man-eating animals occur in certain backward countries on Earth,' put in the Professor. 'Can you do nothing to help these poor wretches?'

Borron said, in effect, that the policy of the High Council on Mino was one of non-interference. They had problems of their own. It was up to every world to work out its own salvation. If once they, the Minoans, started helping other people there would be no end to it; for some of the things that went on in Outer Space, outside their own Solar System, were beyond belief. But that was to be expected, for the planetoids were, after all, only miniature worlds. He had seen worlds so vast that beside them even mighty Jupiter would be no more than a moon.

'Borron is the very man we need for a guide,' declared the Professor. 'He knows his way about. He knows the places that are interesting, those that are safe, and those that are dangerous. He could save us untold time and trouble. Could it be arranged, Vargo?'

Vargo said he was sure it could be arranged, but he failed to understand the Professor's anxiety to rush off into unknown dangers.

The Professor admitted it was sheer curiosity.

'When do you want to start?' asked Vargo.

'The sooner the better,' answered the Professor. 'Now you have the things you don't need us here.'

'You will go first to Mino to speak with the High Council?'

'Of course. If accommodation can be found for us there we should be happy to make it our base while we explore your nearest neighbours.'

'Thus shall it be,' agreed Vargo. He smiled. 'I have a great mind to come with you myself.'

'That would be capital!' cried the Professor. 'Arrange it like that. Which reminds me, I have something to show you.' He then took from his portfolio a sheaf of photographs taken on previous expeditions, including some of the Moon, Venus, and Earth.

To say that Vargo, who knew nothing of photography, was amazed, would be to put it mildly. It was obvious that to him a photograph was more in the nature of a miracle than anything the Earthmen had seen on Mars. And, curiously enough, the pictures that held for him the greatest fascination were those taken on Earth. To Rex it was another example of comparative values. Things which in one place were common, were, to those who had never seen them, wonderful to behold. It really amounted to this: different worlds had discovered different things. Thus, the people on Earth had not developed thought-transference as a means of communication; but they had achieved much the same end by means of radio. On the other hand, to the Minoans, who had lost the art of mechanical invention, a radio set, like the camera, would be a thing to wonder at.

Thinking such thoughts as these, after giving his kitten a saucer of condensed milk, Rex assembled his camp bed and lay down to rest, if not to sleep, for not yet being acclimatized the rarified air affected the action of his heart and lungs, not much, but enough to keep him from the deep sleep he usually enjoyed.

Through the unglazed window, clear and bright, hardly affected by the thin atmosphere of Mars, gleamed a magnificent double star – Earth and its single moon. Somewhere on it, he pondered, was a heather-covered hill from which, so short a while ago, he had gazed up at the star on which he had just made his bed. It was a sobering, almost terrifying thought.

Poor little Earth, he brooded sadly: so busy, so well-meaning, so worried by its troubles, so full of its importance, so proud of its learning that really amounted to so little. He wondered what the people would think when they knew, as one day they must know, the Truth; that they were but a speck of dust in a Universe so stupendous that the puny human brain could not even begin to grasp the beginning or the end of it.

3 To Mino and beyond

Three days later the *Tavona* was on Mino, with the Professor in consultation with the High Council, and Rex, having renewed his friendship with Morino, enlarging his vocabulary of Minoan words. Here it may be said, as might be supposed in view of the Minoan mental development, that the girl was learning English faster than Rex was picking up her language, which was the simpler of the two. Both contained words, particularly nouns, for which the other had no equivalent. Thus, as there were no cats on Mino Rex had to draw a picture of one to explain why the kitten intended for Morino had been left on Mars.

The reason was this. During the morning following their arrival on Mars the animal disappeared, and up to an hour before their departure had not been found. Disappointed, Rex had made a last effort to find it, ending his search on the fringe of the jungle. Calling it by name, 'Snowball', he was delighted to hear it answer, although its hitherto plaintive mew seemed to have taken on a deeper, more vibrant note. When the creature appeared he recoiled in alarm, for not only was it the size of an ordinary full-grown cat but there was a glint in its eye and a feline stealthiness in its step uncomfortably reminiscent of a leopard. When, recovering, he took a step towards it, saying 'puss-puss' in a coaxing voice, he was presented with such a mouthful of fangs, and a snarl of such menacing quality, that he backed hurriedly away.

He knew, of course, what had happened. The creature had obviously eaten something which it had found, alive or dead; at all events something impregnated with the Professor's special insecticide, for this was the effect it had on every living thing in the jungle following the spraying of the mosquitoes during their last visit. Fortunately only a few small creatures had survived.

Hastening to his father he reported what had happened and sought his assistance. But the Professor would not hear of the animal being put into the spaceship, even if that proved possible.

'Are you out of your mind?' he cried. 'The thing might grow in transit to the size of a tiger and then where should we be?'

'Inside a tiger in a spaceship,' murmured Toby.

'Exactly,' agreed the Professor shortly.

So the kitten was left behind.

There had been one other incident even more disturbing than this – at any rate to Rex. Rolto, finding him alone, remarked, 'I hope things go well on Earth.'

'Very well, thank you,' Rex had answered politely and automatically. Then he started. 'How did you learn to speak English?'

Rolto had smiled, the sort of smile that is intended to convey more than words. 'Why not? It is an interesting language, as one would expect of an interesting world.'

Nothing more was said on that occasion but it was enough to make Rex think hard. He went to Vargo and asked him if he had been giving lessons in English to Rolto. Vargo, looking surprised, said no. Whereupon Rex had repeated the conversation to his father. 'I didn't like the way he said it,' he concluded. 'It was almost a hint that he had actually landed on Earth. We know he has often looked at it from a low altitude for he made no secret of it.'

'He might have landed,' answered Tiger thoughtfully. 'There have been rumours of Saucers landing but no one took them seriously. He might have got hold of an English book. Some were left in the *Spacemaster* when we abandoned it. It wouldn't take a man of his intelligence long to work out a language from a book, particularly after hearing us talking.'

'That's true,' agreed Rex. 'Morino already speaks English quite well. It's mostly a matter of memory. I never have to tell her the same word twice. But to come back to Rolto. I have a feeling that although he has given his word to the High Council he hasn't given up hope of helping himself to Earth.'

'I wouldn't worry too much about it,' said Tiger.

Rex tried not to worry, but he thought about it, and later, seeing Rolto standing by his ship he went over to him. 'By the way,' he said, 'I think I ought to warn you not to get too close to Earth.'

'Why?' Rolto arched his eyebrows.

'Because some of the nations there are experimenting with things like high altitude rockets and guided missiles, with the result that explosions in the upper atmosphere are now fairly common and you might collide with one. Besides, with our new radarscopes nothing can approach Earth without being seen.'

'Thank you for the advice,' answered Rolto suavely. 'I will give back the compliment. When you go home say to your College of Science that one step larger with a hydrogen bomb, or should they make a nitrogen bomb, as they now consider, they may surprise themselves by finding no air to breathe, and no water in the big seas. Remembering Kraka, it was to save us all from such a disaster that I wished to go to Earth.' Rolto turned on his heel and would have walked away; but Rex caught him by the sleeve of his tunic.

'How do you know we have made the hydrogen bomb?' he cried.

Rolto hesitated. 'By the colour of its flash and the sonic rays it caused,' he answered smoothly, and went on his way.

Rex didn't know whether to believe him or not, but he

thought there might be something in what he said, for even the scientists were admitting that they might have reached the limit of explosions that could be made without the risk of 'chain-reaction' round the globe; and it was certainly true that the disappearance of Earth would affect every other body in the Solar System.

What a crazy business it all was, he thought bitterly. Here was a beautiful world with a few people jeopardizing its existence, and another lot of people proposing to destroy *them* in order to save it. But then, of course, the people on Earth didn't know that. Perhaps if they did they would forget their own petty squabbles and ambitions. He made a mental note to ask Vargo how much his people knew about the mysterious sonic rays.

But these sombre meditations were put out of Rex's head when Vargo brought the news that the High Council had given permission for the visitors to borrow the *Tavona*, the captain to be the experienced navigator, Borron, and Vargo to act as interpreter.

The Professor announced that they would start on a tour of the planetoids at dawn the following morning, so would Borron and Vargo please proceed with the final arrangements.

Borron had already prepared an itinerary of the planetoids he proposed to visit and produced a chart to illustrate his suggested route, the distance between the several objectives being shown in units of time as registered by an instrument on the panel in the spacecraft. This was standard equipment in all Minoan ships so Rex knew all about it. It was in the manner of a clock, with a dial and a needle, one full circle of the needle representing, according to Rex's watch, about two hours forty minutes of Earthly time. So to work out the distance between objectives at normal cruising velocity was a matter of simple arithmetic. It was no use talking of distance in terms of miles. The time factor was all that mattered.

Naturally, Rex was a little while adapting himself to space-time. As with a foreign language, he found himself, in order to understand its meaning, translating it into his own time of the twenty-four-hour day, regardless of the fact that in space, days and nights did not exist as such. One revolution of the needle round the dial was called, in Minoan, a Vix. The passing of each Vix was marked on a counter, which was in fact the ship's log. Thus, an objective nine Vixes distant would mean a journey of twenty-four hours.

Some of the objectives, as Borron read them out, had fascinating names: Lin; Pallio; Kindor; Jax; Norro; Stontum.

When the time came for leaving, and the spacesuits were put on board, Morino, who had come to see them off, was tearful, much to Rex's embarrassment. He asked her what was the matter, to which she replied: 'I am sad because I shall never see you or my father again.'

'Why not?' asked Rex, in surprise.

'Because,' sobbed Morino, pointing to the sky, 'we know what terrible things happen there.'

'Such as?'

'On Norro there are huge ugly people who cut you in strips, dry you in the sun and eat you for dinner.'

Rex smiled. 'We have fairy tales on Earth, too.'

'But it's true,' cried Morino passionately. 'My father, who goes with you, has seen them. When I was small he would say, if you are naughty I will take you to Norro where you will be cooked on a spit to make a nice mouthful.'

'Don't worry,' consoled Rex. 'He was only trying to frighten you. I'll be back.' So saying, with a wave – for Tiger was calling him – he went in through the airlock. The double doors were closed, and a few minutes later, when the pressure had been adjusted, they were on their way, with Mino shrinking to a ball before their eyes.

Now it was intended that their first call should be made

at Lin, one of the larger planetoids – the one which to Earthly astronomers, the Professor thought, should be Ceres, Vesta, Pallas or Juno; but there was no means of checking this, so they continued to call it by its Minoan name, Lin.

But some time before they reached it the Professor called attention to a singularly brilliant flashing star. Indeed, so bright was it in the blue-black sky, that it was only possible to observe it properly through a piece of tinted plastic-like material provided by Borron, apparently carried for just such a purpose.

Borron announced that the star, or rather, planetoid, was Unkos, a word that simply meant shiner. It was not on the list of places to be visited.

'Why not?' inquired the Professor.

'There is nothing there. Nothing lives,' translated Vargo, when Borron had answered.

'But what causes it to shine like that? Why should it reflect the sun more than others?' the Professor wanted to know. 'Is it ice?'

No, it was not ice, explained Vargo, who went on to say he had heard of the place although he had never been there. It was a good mark for navigators but ships rarely called, having no reason to, as there was no air, water, or life. One gas was present – helium. The rest, he thought, was what he had heard the Professor call glass.

'Then it should be worth a visit,' declared the Professor.

Borron and Vargo held a brief discussion, at the end of which Vargo said they would go there. The reason for the hesitation was certain unusual dangers, one of which was the glare, which was so dazzling from close range that an approach could only be made from the sunless side. Even there it was not dark, for the reflections were carried right round the globe, as presently they would see for themselves. Another danger was, the glass was still cracking as the outer skin became colder.

'But why should that happen to one particular planetoid?' inquired the Professor.

Again Vargo explained. When this particular portion of Kraka had been torn away by the explosion that destroyed that planet it must have consisted chiefly of sand. In passing near the sun on its original orbit the tremendous heat had fused this to form glass. Later, a sunburst had flung it far out into a new orbit, where, in the icy vacuum, the glass had hardened, cracked and split, as they would see.

'Each face of glass would of course act as a reflector,' put in Toby.

'Quite so,' said the Professor. 'It is understandable, particularly when one recalls that when the first experimental atom bomb was let off on an American desert the surface of the sand was afterwards found to be partly glass.'

Borron spoke to Vargo, who again translated. 'Borron says he knows of a similar world to this, but there the surface is ice, not glass. What happened was the fault of the people who lived on it. They were clever, and being short of water on one side of their globe, with much ice on the other side, they decided to make an explosion to tilt the world and bring the ice in a more direct line with the sun. The idea was good, but it was badly managed. The explosion was too big and there was more ice on the Pole than they knew. This great mass melted in a moment and rushed across the world, over-whelming everything and everybody, to fill a great depression on the other side. This caused the world to wobble, and presently overbalance, so that it fell into a new orbit, farther from the sun, where the water again froze. Now everything is covered with a thick skin of ice. Such is the legend, and it may be true, for Borron says he has stood on the ice, and looking down seen the people in it, just as they were on the day they died.'

The Professor nodded pensively. 'Something of the sort

may once have happened on Earth, to account for the great herds of mammoths that are frozen in the Siberian tundra. They, too, are perfectly preserved, and their tusks, which the natives dig out, have been the main source of ivory for generations, and are to this day.'

'That's what comes of tinkering with the thing you're standing on,' joked Tiger.

Vargo did not smile. Apparently to him the subject was not one for humour. From the experiences of his people in space no doubt he knew how little interference was needed to do tremendous damage. It was, reflected Rex, a lesson that the people on Earth had yet to learn, for they were getting clever – perhaps too clever. The trouble was, it seemed that one mistake only was allowed. There was no second chance.

By this time the glare of Unkos was becoming almost painful to the eyes, and it was a relief when Borron put the planetoid between them and the sun. Even so, the sphere still cast off a mysterious glow, mostly green and blue.

Vargo said if they intended to leave the ship it was time they were getting into their spacesuits, which they proceeded to do, carefully testing the controls and adjusting the pressure. This meant from now on the Earth party would be able to converse only with each other, for not having the power of thought-transference, they had to rely on radio, which the Minoans, not needing it, did not possess. However, this would not prevent Vargo from conveying simple messages by his strange power; but they would not be able to reply.

The spectacle that greeted Rex's eyes as they made a cautious approach to the glittering planetoid surpassed anything he could have imagined. He would have said it was possible to visualize a world of glass by mentally magnifying a glass marble a million times; but the limits of his imagination would have fallen far short of reality. He had expected to find a flat surface: but the surface of Unkos was anything but flat. Not only had the glass hardened in mighty sweeping undulations, as if a rolling ocean had been arrested suddenly in motion, but it was split and cracked in all directions to form a chaos of terrifying chasms.

Here, thought Rex, was not only a lifeless world but one that would remain dead for ever. Air might one day return; and perhaps water; but nothing, not even the lowest form of plant life, could put down roots in glass. Phobos, that little moon of Mars, was utterly sterile; but there was soil, and only water and an atmosphere were needed to bring back life. Unkos was large in comparison, how large could more or less be judged by the slight curve of the horizon.

It is not to be supposed that the glass was all the clear transparent product known on Earth as window glass. Far from it. Much of it appeared to be cloudy, even opaque. The basic colours varied from pale green, through blue, to deep violet; but where the glass had split it blazed with all the colours of the spectrum, like a tangle of rainbows. The colours illuminated the inside of the ship as if with neon lights.

Rex was still staring, spellbound, when a soft jar told him they had landed. He looked down, and was instantly seized by a spasm of vertigo, as if he had found himself standing on the lip of a precipice. The globe was not transparent, as he was presently to realize, but the skin at the point where they had touched down was so clear that he might have been gazing into deep blue water.

Borron raised a hand and they followed him into the air-lock chamber, from where, presently, they stepped out on to the hard surface of the glazed world. Walking was difficult and somewhat dangerous, for a slip might have resulted in broken bones; so it was with slow, deliberate steps that they followed their guide to a point from which they could look down into the nearest abyss. Rex looked into it and gasped.

What he saw was so far beyond belief that he could only stare helplessly.

The fissure might have been two hundred yards across, but in depth it seemed to go down to the core of the globe, or at any rate to the limit of the glass. His eyes followed the glittering cliffs down to the bottom, where something seemed to be happening. There, he thought, it must still be in a molten state, for as he watched he saw an enormous bubble blown, presumably a glass bubble, which, as it broke away and started to rise, must have been filled with gas, possibly helium. It didn't reach the top. About halfway up it burst in a shower of crystals. By that time another bubble was forming, to do exactly the same thing.

In a dazed sort of way Rex wondered how long this incredible phenomenon had been going on, and for how long the blow-hole, like the crater of a volcano, would continue to produce bubbles.

He started back in alarm as a great mass of glass broke away from the wall of the chasm, and splintering to a thousand fragments went hurtling down into the cauldron.

He was turning to speak to Tiger, to ask him what he thought of it all, when he saw Borron stare across the flat expanse on which they stood, throw up his arms and start for the ship at a speed that could only mean danger. Staring in the same direction he saw the reason. A new crack was opening in the glass, widening as it moved towards the spot on which they stood, flinging dagger-like splinters to the left and right.

Rex's cry of horror sent them all slipping and sliding towards the ship. It was close, and the outer airlock door was open, but even so Rex thought they would be too late. And so they would have been had not the crack, evidently encountering some obstruction and taking the line of least resistance, suddenly struck off at an angle.

The ship left the ground while they were still in the airlock chamber.

All Borron had to say, when, presently, inside the ship, still pale from shock, they divested themselves of their space-suits, was: 'Unkos is a dangerous place.'

Rex couldn't have agreed more.

4 The unlucky land of Lin

The next port of call – or world of call – on Borron's chart was Lin, and the *Tavona* sped on towards it forthwith, for there was now neither day nor night, only a shadow when one of the many minor planetoids happened to be between the spaceship and the sun. The effect produced was a half-light in the manner of an eclipse, the smaller body sometimes being visible as a black spot, large or small according to its distance from them, against the face of the sun.

Rex took the opportunity to put in some sleep, for the absence of night did not prevent him from becoming tired at the usual regular intervals.

He awoke to learn that the ship was proceeding slowly and with caution, the reason being that across their line of flight there was a trail of debris left by a disintegrating asteroid some time in the past. As Vargo explained, this particular debris, having been cast off in a neutralized gravitational zone, had to remain there until it was disturbed by a comet or meteor which, hurling it or dragging it into the gravitational zone of a planet or planetoid, would, so to speak, clear the air. The stuff would do no damage to the body on which it fell provided there was an atmosphere. This would cause it to become incandescent with heat by friction and disappear before reaching the ground. In other words it would become a cluster of 'shooting stars'.

This Great Barrier Reef in space, as the Professor called it, was a hazard that would not have been expected had they not been told of it. A spaceship colliding with it at speed would certainly not survive the shock of the collision. However, regular space pilots knew all about it, Vargo assured them, and took care to avoid it.

Watching, they saw the reef appear as a smudge across the sky. At the Professor's request Borron took them close. But as a spectacle it was not particularly interesting, comprising only dust, stones and rock. It merely looked unnatural and slightly ridiculous to see such things stationary with nothing to support them. All heavenly bodies were in exactly the same sort of suspension, of course, but in the case of the planets their size made the phenomenon less spectacular.

The *Tavona* continued on its way, and soon afterwards Borron was able to point to the objective. He had a long conversation with Vargo, who then explained.

'Borron thinks you should know something of this place so that you will not be surprised by what you see. You asked to see unusual sights, and for that reason only he put this place on the list, for, while it is large it is not beautiful, and it serves no useful purpose The atmosphere is very strong, and for that reason you may at first be sick. There is too much salt. Salt is on everything and in everything, including the water, which is therefore undrinkable to us. The men here are small and friendly. They can drink the water. Lizards live in the water. There is nothing else. Only men and lizards, very big lizards. As there is nothing else to eat the men live on the lizards and the lizards live on the men. To escape from the lizards the men must make their houses in the trees. These, like everything, are white with salt; but if you rub the salt from the leaves they are green. Lin is a world of salt. Sometimes some is taken to where there is none, presents being given for it, for which reason the men like to see a ship come. They have nothing to lose, not even their land, which no one would have as a gift. This is what Borron has asked me to tell you.'

'A world of salt,' muttered the Professor. 'Strange, but not really remarkable when one remembers that at home all our large bodies of water contain salt, as does much of the land, to a greater or lesser degree. Tell us, Vargo, why do these men stay here?'

'They have lived in a world of salt for so long that they cannot live anywhere else. Where they came from originally, or how they got here, no one knows. But now they must have salt, much salt, or they die. They may soon die anyway, for always they become fewer and the lizards more. In the end the lizards will win, only to die of starvation when there are no men left to eat.'

'But have these men no form of cultivation that they must rely on lizard meat?' inquired the Professor.

'We have given them seeds, but nothing will grow in the salt earth except a hard grass and one sort of tree such as you never saw before.'

'Have they no fish in their water?'

'They do not know, and cannot find out, for they dare not go near the water except to fetch some for drinking; and this is so dangerous because of the lizards that many men must go together, and even then some are killed.'

'How do these men kill the lizards?' inquired Tiger.

'They have spears, but they are not good, for which reason we bring some, as we have today. But they lose them when they are torn from their hands by lizards which, when they are wounded, rush back to the water.'

'What these fellers want,' put in Toby, 'is a rifle or two.'

Tiger, who had a rifle on board, put it in a convenient place, and they all watched the little planet, now drawing near, with mounting interest. Not that much could be seen, for there was a heavy layer of cloud. The ship passed through this and the strange new world lay exposed to view.

Had it not been for Vargo's description Rex would have wondered what they were approaching, for the surface was a variegated pattern of black and white, the black areas presumably being water. There was no big land mass, only a vast archipelago of islands. There was far more water than land. Had he not known of the salt he would have thought they were looking on an Arctic zone, the white being caused by frost rather than snow, for as the ship went nearer the white turned out to be pale grey.

Vargo said that Borron, who spoke the Linian language, had been informed that there was a legend among the people that long ago they had travelled from island to island in boats: but that was no longer possible on account of the water-lizards. Now the people had to remain where they were.

To Rex the scene presented was a world as hideous as could be imagined; but the Professor made no secret of his delight, for, as he declared, Lin supported his theory that life could exist in any conditions, no matter how impossible they might seem to those who dwelt on worlds where conditions were entirely different.

Rex observed that they were dropping down on one of the larger islands, although its area could not have been more than twenty square miles. The uniform colouration made it difficult to see anything clearly, but he made out a stand of trees, not a very large stand, at one end of the island. It had at one time been larger, but all round the outside of the wood – if wood is the right word – the trees had been smashed and splintered as if swept by a hurricane. Presently he was to see the sort of hurricane that had been responsible. As for the trees themselves, they were something in the nature of a cross between a palm and a monkey-puzzle; but it was a species unknown to him. Everything was grey, but he could see huts in the trees, with rough timber platforms running from one to the other.

As soon as the *Tavona* touched down, on an open area less than a hundred yards from the trees, the place came to life when what appeared to be a swarm of grey apes descended from the tree-top village with astonishing agility and raced, shouting, towards the ship. Borron was not in the least intimidated, and passing the word that spacesuits would not be required threw open the double doors of the airlock chamber.

Knowing what he knew Rex was not particularly surprised by what he saw, particularly as he recalled that even Earth could boast a race of pygmies, in the West African jungle; but that is not to say he was not startled. The men were men. Of that there was no doubt, for aside from their appearance, which was not too far removed from normal, they kept up a chatter of conversation. Their skins were white, as was their hair and beards, although how far this was due to an incrustation of white, crystalline powder, presumably salt, was not easy to determine. They were short in stature, none being more than four feet tall, and their arms were abnormally long, as might have been expected in a race of tree dwellers. Their clothing was standard, and comprised a long shirt and high boots of what looked like grey crocodile hide. Every man carried at least one spear, some several.

Rex followed the others out to find himself in an atmosphere that was both close and heavy It had a slightly suffocating effect, but that was all. The Linians did not seem in the least surprised to see them, although this, too, was to be expected, as they had often been visited by spaceships. The women, distinguishable by long hair, remained near or at the doors of their huts, which were built either in the trees themselves or on platforms high off the ground between them. These were of a dirty grey colour. Indeed, this was the colour of the entire landscape and everything on it. Nothing more drab and miserable could have been imagined, and Rex was sorry for the poor wretches who had to endure it, although, to be sure, they seemed cheerful enough, knowing nothing better.

'If the people on Earth could see this place they'd be well satisfied with what *they've* got,' remarked Rex, watching the Professor, with his spectacles on the end of his nose, taking some snapshots of the Linians, who were afterwards rewarded, to their almost hysterical delight, with a bag of caramels. Some rushed off and brought back some small skin bags of salt, apparently all they had to offer.

'I hope the Professor won't stay here much longer,' went on Rex, to Tiger, who was taking the opportunity to have a smoke. 'I'm feeling a bit sick, and my mouth's as dry as a chip.'

'That will be the salt,' answered Tiger. 'The stuff is in the air as well as in everything else. I think we've seen all there is to see.'

In this, however, he was wrong. He must have forgotten the lizards!

They were all reminded of the other inhabitants of the planetoid when Toby called attention to several long white objects moving swiftly across the inky surface of the water about a quarter of a mile away. A Linian scout must have been on the watch, for there was a shrill yell, and in a moment the little men were streaking for their elevated houses.

'The lizards,' said Vargo simply, pointing.

Still no one paid much attention, except perhaps the Professor, who focused his glasses on them. 'My word!' he exclaimed. 'This is interesting. Very interesting indeed.'

The beasts may have been interesting, but Rex could have found a more descriptive word as the first of the creatures shot on to the dry land like a fast boat running ashore, and without pause came lumbering on up one of the several broad tracks which Rex had supposed to be man-made roads, but now had reason to think were game-tracks; or rather, lizard tracks.

With the others following more slowly the leading lizard came on at a speed which Rex, who had always regarded the lizard as a slow-moving reptile, could hardly believe. The forward movement was not so much a gallop as a glide, and the reason for this, as he observed as the beast drew nearer, was because it had not the usual four legs, but several. These moved so fast, in the style of those of a centipede, that he found it difficult to count them; but he thought there were ten. About thirty feet long, the creatures were not unlike crocodiles, although here he realized that he was falling back on an Earthly name to describe something which did not exist on Earth. In colour the brutes were, like everything else, a pallid white, which for some reason made them look particularly horrible.

'They're some pretty beauties, I must say,' remarked Toby. 'They look halfway between a dragon and a centipede. Quite wizardly in their own way. From the way the tree-top boys took evasive action they must be scared rigid.'

'Back to the ship,' ordered Vargo.

'Just a minute! Let's watch this. What are they going to do?' said Tiger, loading his rifle.

'They will attack the men,' answered Vargo. 'And if we stay here they will attack us, too.'

'But the men are in the trees,' the Professor pointed out.

'They are in the trees, but that does not make them safe,' returned Vargo. 'You will see. You are watching a struggle for survival in its final stages.'

Such a sight as Rex never expected to see was now presented. The leading lizard, reaching the trees, chose one, and rearing up on its hind legs began tearing at the trunk with its teeth and claws in a bestial fury that was dreadful to behold.

'Great Heaven!' cried the Professor. 'He'll have that tree down.'

This was so obviously going to happen that no one denied it. But the uncouth beast was not to have things all its own way. With an incredible din of yelling and screaming, spears began to rain down on it from above – not that they seemed to be having much effect. Some did not even penetrate the brute's hide, but glanced off harmlessly. What amazed Rex was the courage of the little men, for far from abandoning the tree being attacked they came to it from all sides. What was going to happen when the tree fell, as presently it must, was something Rex preferred not to think about. Salt crystals, dislodged by the shaking, fell like a steady rain of diamonds to give a final touch of fantasy to the picture.

'In Africa I once saw the Masai take on a lion with their spears, but this beats anything I ever heard of,' remarked Toby. 'What does that chap think he's going to do?'

Rex stared as a little old man, with a rope coiled over one arm, started down towards the beast's slavering jaws. The noise was indescribable.

Toby's question was answered by the man himself. Halting only a yard from the monstrous face, with wonderful dexterity he threw a loop round the jaws. This was instantly pulled taut by the men above, thus closing the jaws. The little man, taking another rope, now jumped to the ground and tried to get a noose round the lizard's tail.

'He's mad!' cried Rex.

'They must kill the lizard for food or die of starvation,' said Vargo simply.

'Well, that's one way of getting the Sunday joint, but I should have to be mighty hungry before I tried it,' said Tiger.

The old man succeeded in his purpose and dashed round the tree with the obvious intention of securing the tail to it. Speed was necessary, for the other lizards were getting close. At this juncture, however, the business took a turn that was obviously not in the programme. The tree, weakened by the attack made on it, began to bend under the beast's weight, and the broken trees which Rex had thought to be the result of a hurricane were explained. This frightful business must, he realized, be a common occurrence.

Over went the tree with a crash, taking the beast with it. The men who had been on it fell off like ripe plums. The strain on the ropes being released the lizard tore itself free, and bellowing with rage went after the old man who had played the leading part in the drama. It would have caught him, too, had not Tiger taken a hand.

'If our little St George can't kill his dragon I'd better see what I can do,' said he. Raising his rifle he took quick aim and fired.

Making a terrible noise the beast reared up, tearing at its side. Again Tiger's rifle cracked, and this time the bullet must have found a vital spot, for the beast fell on its back and lay kicking. The Linians did not wait for it to die, but with shrieks of triumph fell on it with their spears. When its struggles ceased the men began a war-dance round their hereditary foe. This did not last long, however, and in a few minutes the entire tribe, men, women and children, were hacking their enemy to pieces.

'A pretty example of nature in the raw,' remarked the Professor, as they stood watching the gory spectacle. 'Before we criticize we should do well to remember that our ancestors on Earth must have gone through a period of this sort of thing.'

'They survived. Here they look like losing. I wonder why?' said Toby.

'I think I can answer that,' rejoined the Professor. 'Our ancestors were better armed. They knew how to work flint, and later, bronze. The spears and choppers these fellows are using appear to be singularly futile, as if they have no points, or edges.'

It so happened that a man came over with a horrid lump of flesh and offered it, apparently as a present. The Professor took his spear from him and adjusting his spectacles examined the point. He scratched it with a thumbnail. Then, taking out his penknife, he made a groove. The face he turned to those watching him broke into a whimsical smile. 'Observe the irony of fate, gentlemen!' he exclaimed. 'These silly fellows have chosen the most useless of all metals for the most important of all work, which is to preserve their lives.'

'What is it?' asked Tiger.

'Gold.'

'*Gold!*'

'Yes, and fine gold too.'

'There is no other metal here,' explained Vargo, who was listening.

'That's a joke,' said Toby.

'I don't know,' put in Tiger. 'Talking of ancestors, if legend is true the Druids used golden sickles to cut the mistletoe in their sacred oaks.'

The Professor chuckled. 'Sheer nonsense, my dear fellow. In the first place, in Britain gold does not exist, and never has existed, in sufficient quantity to make tools. We find flint and tin and bronze, but not gold weapons. Secondly, if gold had existed it would not take an edge to cut wood. And finally, oak is one of the few trees on which you will never find mistletoe. I'm sorry to spoil a pretty story but we must stick to the truth. Civilization has never enough gold. Here the tragedy of these poor people is, they have nothing else. To them one rifle would be worth more than all their gold. Not that I think these people would ever make much progress towards a better life.'

'Shall I give them a rifle?' suggested Tiger.

'That would only hasten their extermination. According to Vargo they can live nowhere else but here. At present they die one by one. Give them a rifle and they will, by destroying their food supply, die in numbers from starvation.'

'I'll see they are not hungry for a little while,' said Tiger, and advancing towards the herd of lizards coming slowly up the track killed six of them – to the great joy of the Linian population.

At this point Rex was sick.

'I'm beginning to feel the effects of this salt-laden atmosphere myself,' admitted the Professor. 'Our visit here has been most enlightening, but I think we have seen all that is worth seeing, so as time is precious we might leave these wretches to enjoy their disgusting lunch and move on to a more salubrious planet.'

They returned to the ship.

5 Worlds of wonder

As the *Tavona* resumed its tour Rex could not help thinking about the unfortunate people on the world now dropping away below them. The more he thought about their wretched plight the harder he tried to think of a solution to their problem of life or death. In such conditions there could be no hope of progress.

He felt sure that if the lizards could be brought under control it ought to be possible to introduce an alternative staple article of food. There should be vegetables that would tolerate the saline soil. The coconut palm, for instance. On the Pacific islands that most useful tree often grew with its roots in the sea. The water might produce fish. If there was none there already they could be introduced from elsewhere – perhaps from Earth. In some countries salt fish was one of the chief articles of food.

He conveyed these thoughts to the Professor, saying that if the lizards could be exterminated and fish put in their place the Linians would soon learn how to catch them. If they hadn't fish hooks already they could soon make some.

The Professor smiled wryly. 'You can be sure that they know nothing of fish hooks, and as for inventing them ... Always remember, Rex, the more primitive form of human life the slower is the process of invention and development. On Earth the modern fish hook may have taken a million years to produce. At first, and for how long we don't know, hooks were made of thorns, chipped flint and carved shells. These are sometimes found in ancient tombs.

'The big jump forward came when, about six thousand

years ago, a genius of his time made a hook of bent metal. Copper. It was a great and wonderful invention for the human race, for it must have increased enormously the supply of fish for food. But two thousand years more were to elapse before another man had a brainwave and put a barb on his hook. Again we know that from tombs of the period. Think of it! From the first flight to the modern aeroplane, from radio to television, took a mere fifty years; but from a plain hook to one with a barb required two thousand. The invention of the barbed hook was certainly of greater benefit to humanity. You can't eat aeroplanes, and television won't save you if you are starving; but the barbed hook again stepped up the supply of fish for the hungry crowds in the public markets of the old world.' The Professor popped a caramel into his mouth.

'So you see,' he concluded, 'a simple thing like a fish hook provides us with a good example of the time factor in early technical invention. To an Ancient Briton a barbed copper hook would have been worth more than all the gold in Lin, where I should be very surprised indeed to find one. But never mind. We'll save them a few thousand years of head-ache by giving them some hooks – when there are fish to catch. I will think about it.'

The next port of call on Borron's route was Norro, a world of strong men; but Vargo came over to say that as they would pass some lesser planetoids on the way the Professor might like to see them. Not that there was much of interest. One was entirely covered with water. Another was clothed in tall grass, and another was the place of ice of which they had been told; where the people in attempting to tilt their world to their advantage had melted the polar ice-caps and so destroyed themselves. If they called there spacesuits would have to be worn.

Although Vargo used the word spacesuits there was no

actual equivalent in his own language, the term in Minoan, literally translated, being air-holding tube. The word for space was hardly ever used. Travel automatically meant space travel, this method of transporation being as normal as sea travel on Earth.

The Professor said he would like to see as many planetoids as possible, large or small, and Vargo passed on the information to Borron – although he, and the entire crew for that matter – by reason of their high intelligence were already able to speak English well enough to keep pace with ordinary conversation.

'One thing has been puzzling me for some time,' the Professor told Vargo. 'This area of space seems to be entirely free from meteors and comets.'

Vargo appeared to be slightly surprised by this observation. 'It is not entirely free. Some come in from outer space, but not often; and we rely on the Watch Squadron to give us warning of the likelihood of such visitations anywhere and at any time. For the rest, Borron knows the areas where such things occur commonly and takes care to avoid them. Ships are sometimes lost, nevertheless, either from collisions with meteors on a course normally free from them, or from an error of calculation on the part of the navigator. Watch how our position is checked and cross-checked constantly with the stars. Borron knows exactly where he is. He must, otherwise we might easily become lost and spend the rest of our lives trying to find our way home to Mino. That once happened to a ship of the Remote Survey Fleet. It lost its bearings in a cloud of meteoric dust and hope for the crew had long been given up when it returned. They had some strange adventures those men, for running out of even the emergency rations they had to land for food and water on unknown worlds. Only three of the original crew of seven survived.'

Rex wished the Professor had not raised this disturbing

subject. 'It wouldn't be easy to lose your way?' he suggested.

'It can happen very easily,' declared Vargo. 'I doubt if you, alone, would ever find your way back to Earth, now that it is one of a million stars, dwarfed by bodies that are nearer to us.'

Rex said no more. He felt it was better not to know too much about these things. Anyway, at this juncture Borron pointed out to him such a world as he never expected to see. There was nothing but water. The globe was completely inundated. Rex found that a world of water was almost beyond comprehension, never mind imagination. Nowhere, he thought, could there be a more graphic illustration of that incomprehensible power, gravity. Even allowing for the fact that water was merely a mixture of gases its weight was such that it must always run down any incline. On this small planetoid the slope was plain to see, yet the water did not run off. Gravity, obviously, slight though it must be on such a small body, was still sufficient to hold the water in place.

Yet, pondered Rex, if it did run off, where would it run? Looked at like that the whole thing became ridiculous. The same argument could be applied to the great oceans of the Earth, of course, where water could be seen bending over the horizon, so to speak. It did not run off; nor did it flood the land on the lower side of the globe. But in that case, reasoned Rex, the pull of gravity was proportionate to the size of the globe. No wonder the ancients refused to accept the theory that the world was round, saying that if it were the water would run off.

The planetoid was not a solid ball of water although it looked like it, Vargo said. The water was probably shallow, although as landing was impossible the depth was not known. Their old records said that there had once been land – points of rock. These must have sunk out of sight. They had not been washed away, for without an atmosphere there could be no wind, and as they could see for themselves the water lay like a sheet of glass, without a ripple. There never could be a ripple – unless the little planet one day managed to collect some air, which was not impossible.

Rex wondered if there were any fish in the waters of this watery world. No one knew, and without some sort of landing device no one ever would know. For the same reason it had been impossible to take a sample of the water in order to ascertain its chemical contents.

As they stood gazing down on what appeared to be an endless sheet of burnished steel the Professor reminded them that on Earth the lost continent of Atlantis had sunk beneath the waves; and a rise in the present water level of a mere fifty feet would leave only the tops of mountains, and a few high plateaux, showing.

The ship went on its way. There was another long silence, broken at last by Vargo, who said they were now approaching Jax, the world of grass.

'Do you mean nothing else grows except grass?' asked Rex.

'Yes. It grows everywhere except where the rock comes through the ground.'

'Is there no other form of life?' inquired the Professor.

'There may be. Borron does not know. To explore is not possible, so tall and strong and thick is the grass. I have not been to the place myself,' explained Vargo, 'but Borron says the edges of the grass are so sharp that they cut like knives.'

'Sounds like some sort of cactus,' opined Tiger.

'Soon you will see, for Borron is looking for a landing ground,' replied Vargo.

Through his window Rex looked down upon a globe of emerald green, broken only here and there by ridges of rock and an occasional plateau, towards one of which the *Tavona* was sinking. The surface looked safe enough for a landing anywhere, but his aviation experience told him that from an altitude an apparently inviting surface could be a death trap. A field of tall green corn has often overturned a pilot who took it for a well-grazed meadow.

The ship went on down and presently scratched its landing feet on a small island of what looked like limestone in an ocean of vivid green. In the absence of an atmosphere there could be no wind, and as there was no wind the sea of grass remained as motionless as a picture. So closely packed grew the grass that it was possible only to see the tops, and for that reason the depth of the sea, otherwise the height of the grass, could not be ascertained. There was not a movement anywhere.

Rex would have said there was no point in getting out of the ship; they could see everything there was to see from where they were. Apparently the Professor thought otherwise, for with his usual enthusiasm he started to get into his spacesuit. The others followed his example, and after the usual delay they went through the airlock to stand, somewhat unsteadily, for their weight was negligible, on the surface of the planetoid Jax.

After a thoughtful survey of the monotonous panorama the Professor, swaying slightly, made his way cautiously down the nearest slope with the obvious intention of examining the grass from close quarters. Rex went with him, while the others, presumably thinking that the reward was not likely to be worth the trouble, remained where they were, watching. Not that there appeared to be the slightest risk of danger.

It was soon evident to Rex that the grass was in fact a sort of bamboo which grew even more tightly packed than wheat in a cornfield. He imagined it would be difficult, if not impossible, to force a passage through it. But what amazed him more than anything was the height of the stuff in comparison with the thickness of the stalk. The growth was not less than twenty feet high, yet the stalk was no thicker than a knitting needle. Such a phenomenon would be impossible on Earth where wind or rain, or both, would lay the crop flat. But here, apparently, there was neither wind nor rain, so all the stems had to support was its slender leaves, and, near the top, a white ball that was, Rex assumed, the blossom or the fruit. In this, however, he was mistaken, as he was soon to learn.

As he stood still, wondering whence came the water to keep the growth alive, he became aware of a faint humming noise, like the twang of a banjo string; but the curious thing was, instead of dying away, or being sustained, it seemed to increase slowly in volume. Where the sound came from, or what caused it, he could not work out. Not that he paid any great attention to it. He saw the Professor take one of the thin leaves between his fingers and press as if to bend it, but it snapped as if made of glass.

An instant later he was confronted by another mystery when, from an outer stalk, one of the objects he had taken to be seed pods broke off and floated at an angle towards the Professor. How could it do that, he wondered, if there was no atmosphere? In such conditions, no matter how light it might be, surely it should drop directly to the ground? The buzzing noise grew louder, but still no thought of danger entered his head. What was there to be afraid of in a world of grass and a few balls of fluff?

Only when more and more broke off without apparent cause or reason did he become uneasy; but it was not until one of them, landing near the Professor's feet, burst open to discharge a mass of ant-like insects, that the truth hit him and fear seized him by the throat.

'Look out, Professor,' he cried shrilly, and turning, began to scramble back up the rocky slope. Halfway he looked to see if the Professor was following, and at the sight that met his gaze he let out a strangled cry of horror. The air was full of the white fluffy balls and the ground was a crawling carpet of insects. Leading the attacking army were some extra large ones, a good two inches long. Before them fled the Professor, making prodigious leaps in the nearly weightless conditions.

Above, Tiger was beckoning frantically – not that Rex needed any urging. He reached the spacecraft first and scrambled inside. The others followed, and the door was slammed just as the black tide reached it.

Not until the ship was in motion and spacesuits removed did anyone speak. Then the Professor said: 'I ought to be ashamed of myself for breaking my own rule of taking nothing for granted. Those spiders may or may not have been venomous, but had we got them on our persons it's hard to see how we could have avoided bringing them into the ship with us. I really must be more careful.'

'The whole place was a death-trap,' declared Tiger. 'A ship landing anywhere but on the rock would have a thin time on Spider Island.'

'The spiders certainly ruled the roost,' remarked Toby.

'I doubt if they had anything to rule – except themselves,' opined the Professor drily. 'Their strength lay in their numbers and organization. One finds the same thing to a lesser extent on earth, in Africa and South America, so there's nothing particularly astonishing about it. Let us not forget the lesson.'

The ship sped on to its next objective, which was understood to be Pallio, the world that had been upset by its population and was now a mass of blue ice.

A number of very small planetoids were seen on the way, but the ship did not stop, Vargo saying that they were merely barren rocks. These tiny bodies were much too small to be observed from Earth, for which reason, as the Professor observed, the total number of planetoids had been greatly underestimated by the astronomers. Instead of the three thousand or so that had been given names or numbers it began to look as if there might be thirty thousand, or even fifty thousand, large or small. That being so, there could be no question of exploring all of them.

Pallio appeared as a glittering blue-white star in a coal-black sky, sometimes to be briefly extinguished as one of the smaller planetoids passed between it and the sun. The sun, it should be said, was still obviously master of the System, but on account of distance was, in comparison with Earthly observation, reduced in size.

The objective became larger and more brilliant as Borron made his usual cautious approach, although at the finish there was no need to seek a landing ground, for the surface appeared to be as smooth as a marble.

'You may not be aware of it,' said the Professor thoughtfully, 'but what has happened here could happen on Earth should our own world tilt farther on its axis and move to a greater distance from the sun. There is enough snow and ice at the Poles to inundate the present dry land except for the highest mountains, which would then become islands in one vast ocean of water. Should that water freeze, Earth would appear as what you see before you – on a much larger scale, of course.'

'Could an explosion cause Earth to tilt?' asked Rex.

'Of course, if of sufficient force,' answered the Professor. 'After all, that is what happened here. A large comet, or a planetoid, passing close, would have the same effect.'

Rex did not pursue the subject. Over him again crept that awful feeling of insecurity in the immensity of the Universe.

The ship settled on the frozen globe as lightly as a thistle seed. Spacesuits were donned. The doors were opened and they stepped out on to hard blue ice. Not a mark broke its surface. The ice ran on and on in every direction to a clean-cut curving horizon.

54

It was Borron who, by pointing, reminded them of what they had come to see. He pointed down. Rex looked, and for the first time in his life found himself gazing, without being airborne, at a landscape under his feet. The effect was much the same as if he had looked down from a low-flying aircraft on a misty day; but here there was no movement. The water – or rather, ice – was not as deep as he had thought it would be, and he could see everything distinctly – trees, fields and houses. Preserved in ice, all remained exactly as they were when they were overwhelmed, and would remain, presumably, until the end of time, unless another move caused the ice to melt. Pallio was, in fact, nothing but a vast refrigerator.

Again conscious of a feeling of unreality he walked a little way, staring below as a diver might look down into the deep water under him. He saw an animal, a creature like a small cow. Near it, a man, arms outflung, looked up at him.

That was as much as he wanted to see of the nightmarish place, and as he walked back to the ship the Professor's voice came over the radio. 'Excavation here, if it were possible, should yield some startling results.'

Rex agreed, but had no wish to be present at such a project.

They did not stay long. Back in the ship, as they divested themselves of their suits, Vargo remarked, quietly: 'They did that to themselves. Many worlds have been destroyed by the inhabitants.'

'You mean by the scientists,' said Rex coldly.

He was thinking of what some of the scientists on Earth were doing.

6 The peculiar people of Norro

As the *Tavona* continued its tour Rex sank into a reverie that was not entirely happy. He, like most boys of his age, had wanted adventure. He had found it, beyond all reasonable expectation. He had, he felt, found too much. That was the trouble. He was out of his depth. The awful immensity of space, of the Universe, made his brain reel. Such words as eternity and infinity were really beyond human understanding, he told himself. Time and distance no longer meant anying. A million years, a million miles – what were they? They could not even be imagined, let alone appreciated.

It was one thing to sit at home and consider the stars but a different thing altogether to be among them. The Solar System that had seemed so vast he now knew to be but a grain of sand in the Sahara of the mighty heavens: a dot in the Milky Way: and the Milky Way, with its millions of stars, was but one constellation, one galaxy, in yet more millions. Yes, it was too much. He began to wish he had stayed at home.

Not so the Professor, engaged in enthusiastic argument with Tiger and Toby over what they had seen. What conditions, asked the Professor, had produced the various forms of life, animal and vegetable? Was it an unequal distribution of the elements of which the Universe was composed? What part did gravity play? Light? Temperature?

Rex didn't know, and at this juncture he didn't particularly care. What perhaps depressed him more than anything were the terrifying things that could happen to a world. He had seen some of them. Would his own fair Earth one day become a ball of ice, or glass, or perhaps disappear completely in a wisp of smoke? The thought that if this did not happen in a celestial accident it might be caused by inquisitive scientists living on the planet made his blood boil. To the deuce with them and their monstrous explosions. Why couldn't they leave things alone?

These morbid thoughts were interrupted when Vargo stepped into the conversation. They were, he said, on the way to Norro, but Borron had doubts about landing there. It was a strange place and he would prefer to leave the decision to them. It was years since Borron had been there, but one of the crew, who had served in the Remote Survey Fleet, and had been there recently, held that it was not safe.

'Is anywhere safe?' asked the Professor drily.

Vargo took the question seriously. He said there were safe places, but reminded the Professor that he had expressed a wish to see the unusual places, and it was with that object that the intinerary had been arranged.

'Then let us go to Norro,' decided the Professor. 'What in particular have we to fear?'

Vargo explained. Norro was a planetoid of some size, one of the largest that had been charted, the reason being, perhaps, it had a comfortable atmosphere. There was water that could be drunk in small quantities, and a rich growth of vegetation that produced grain, fruit and vegetables, although unfortunately most of these were poisonous to anyone not accustomed to them. The people were vegetarian, rather larger than themselves in size and of tremendous strength. Their bodies being covered with fine hair they wore no clothes except girdles of leaves, beautifully woven. They spoke a strange language which no one had been able to learn and lived in holes in the ground.

'Why?' asked the Professor.

'Because there are many animals, all what you call carnivorous. They are the danger.'

'What are these animals?'

'We have no names for them. There are many sorts. All are large and covered with fur, some black, some yellow, some red. They hunt in packs. Sometimes after eating the fallen over-ripe fruit of a certain tree they go mad and tear each other to pieces. The people, who at any time can only go out many together, must then barricade themselves in their holes.'

'What an extraordinary state of affairs,' murmured Tiger. 'How did the animals come to get the upper hand?'

'The people, being vegetarians, never killed them, and so they must have increased out of all proportion. We don't know. That is only what we suppose.'

'Yet the men are strong?'

'Very strong. Fustor, who has been among them, says he has seen one take a nut, which he could not break with a stone, and crush it flat between his fingers.'

'We must get samples of this fruit for analysis, to see from what they derive their strength,' declared the Professor. 'If we knew it would be of benefit at home.'

'I'm not so sure of that,' said Toby softly.

'Anyway, let us go to Norro by all means,' asserted the Professor. 'It promises to be a most interesting port of call. It rather looks, Group-Captain, as if you may need a rifle.'

It was evident when, some time later, they drew near to the big planetoid, all that Vargo had said of its luxuriant verdure was true. Had it not been for a curving horizon they might have been approaching a fertile section of Earth. They saw woods, open plains and lakes, but no seas or rivers. In general the country might best be described as rolling; that is to say, there were low hills but no mountains. No deserts or rocky areas could be seen, the surface everywhere being hidden under a blanket of vegetation, timber or grass. Some small objects could be seen moving on the open places, but whether men or animals could not yet be distinguished.

Borron took the ship to one of the larger plains, which lay at the foot of some sharply rising ground, with deep forest on either side. Very soon it was to turn out that no worse spot could have been chosen, although the Professor might have argued that it was the best spot. From the point of view of observing the state of affairs that prevailed it was certainly a good spot, although when the ship touched down there was not a living creature in sight. But these conditions did not last long.

Vargo checked the test-valve, and satisfied with the result, opened the double doors, slowly, letting in a breath of sweet but cold air that brought with it a faint indefinable aroma which, after the artificial atmosphere in the ship Rex found wonderfully refreshing.

One by one they filed out, Tiger taking his rifle, to stand knee deep in lush grass and a riot of wild flowers none of which Rex was able to recognize. Nothing moved. The air was dead still. Not a sound broke a queer, attentive silence. To Rex, but for a perceptible chill, they might have been standing in an English water-meadow on a summer's day. Indeed, he found it hard to believe that this was not so until his eyes made out some unfamiliar tropical-looking fruits on a nearby tree. What delighted him more than anything was a blue sky overhead, instead of black skies where there was no atmosphere. He had to say to himself, 'I am standing on a star,' in order to convince himself of it.

Suddenly Vargo pointed. All eyes switched to the point indicated. Fifty or so yards away something stirred. A heavy log was being moved aside. Then, from the aperture, stepped a man; a big man, not only tall but broad-shouldered. He had long, yellowish hair, a beard of the same colour, and wore what at first glance appeared to be a tight-fitting camel-hair robe caught in at the waist with a multicoloured kilt. Then, remembering Vargo's description, Rex realized that the robe was in fact hair – not fur, but the sort of hair some men have on their chests, although in this case it covered the entire body. Behind, in the recesses of the hole from which the man had emerged, Rex could see other faces, peering out.

Vargo held up his right hand. The man moved forward. Others followed, slowly, as if not quite sure of themselves, or the new arrivals. And in spite of all that Vargo had said Rex gazed at them with mixed sensations of wonder, compassion, and admiration – the latter because as physical specimens they were magnificent, none being less than seven feet tall.

How this matter would have ended had there been no interruption is a matter for speculation; but when the men were no more than halfway, with the visitors strolling to meet them, there suddenly broke out, at no great distance, such a pandemonium that both parties, after a brief halt, retired, the natives in haste, the visitors more slowly. The source of the sound was not for a minute revealed, but it obviously came from somewhere inside the nearest forest The air vibrated with a terrible roaring, so that to Rex it sounded like nothing so much as feeding time in the lion house at the zoo.

Reaching the door of the ship the visitors stopped to await developments, as did, Rex noticed, the natives, one of whom stood with the log under his arm presumably to block the cave should this become necessary. It was at this point that Rex noticed more cave entrances farther along the bank, with their owners standing just outside, watching and waiting in the manner of rabbits at the entrances to their burrows when a dog appears on the scene. Had the picture not contained elements of tragedy, this reversal of roles, human beings taking the part of rabbits, would not have been without a humorous aspect.

But such thoughts as these were banished from his mind in a flash when the scene burst into life and action as a 'still' photograph might switch to a movie.

From out of the timber, running at unbelievable speed, their long hair flying, came a party of Norroans, making for their homes. That they were flying from some peril was evident, yet they ran without panic, as men who had done the same thing before. They had obviously been gathering fruit, for some still carried baskets, and although certain of the contents were lost in the haste of their flight they did not abandon their loads. Rex admired their courage and tenacity all the more when the pursuit arrived on the scene.

From the trees now burst a pack of animals the like of which he had never imagined, much less seen. Their furry bodies, the size and colour of lions, were those of cats; and had their heads been in keeping there would have been nothing really remarkable about them. But they were not. They were long, with pointed muzzles, like those of wolves; and while the result was a mammal that *might* have occurred on Earth the unfamiliar mixture of cat and dog gave them a particularly horrible appearance.

Clamouring like hounds in full cry they made a noise that was something between a howl and a roar; and again, it was the unnatural quality of this that helped to make the picture one of fantasy rather than reality.

It was soon clear that the horrid pack would claim at least one victim, a man whose greying beard suggested that he was older than the rest, and for that reason had fallen a little behind. Fast overtaking him was the leader of the nightmare beasts.

Rex, who had been spellbound as he watched helplessly,

jumped when his father shouted, 'Mind yourself!' and then dropped on one knee, rifle to shoulder, with the obvious intention of taking a hand. The range was comparatively short, less than a hundred yards, but even so, to hit such a fast-moving target with a single bullet, would, Rex feared, call for finer marksmanship than could be expected in the circumstances. In any case he thought Tiger would be too late to do any good, for only a few feet separated the beast from its prey. But he had reckoned without the man who now treated the spectators to an exhibition of strength and agility that left Rex gasping.

As if realizing that he was about to be overtaken the old man turned in a flash, dropped his basket and crouched, hands in front of him. When the beast sprang, fangs bared, he caught it in mid air, and straightening his legs, hurled it such a distance that Rex could not believe his eyes; for, even taking reduced gravity into account, the beast on Earth would not have weighed less than five hundred pounds. Yet the man had flung it aside as if it might have been a kitten.

For a split second, as it landed, it offered a sitting target. Tiger's rifle cracked. The brute reared up, obviously hit; but it came on, limping, after the man, who, apparently noticing the spacecraft for the first time, and perceiving that it was nearer than his burrow, turned towards it. Tiger fired again. The beast sprang high, fell, and lay kicking, whereupon its companions instantly rushed upon it in the manner of wolves and began tearing it to pieces. This brief delay undoubtedly saved the man, who reached the ship just ahead of his pursuers. They dragged him in.

Borron, who must have been watching, now acted with great presence of mind; for the doors were open, and for a few seconds there was danger of at least one of the brutes getting inside. Indeed, in a desperate spring, one got its forepaws on the step; but Tiger fired into the slavering mouth and it fell off. The energy then came on and the ship swung clear of the ground.

'All right! Hold her there, Borron!' yelled Tiger, when the ship had risen perhaps fifty feet, with the doors still open, for the need to close them had passed. Then lying down, he began, one by one, to liquidate the howling pack. As Toby remarked, it would have been hard to imagine a more fantastic spectacle. The final touch was provided when the ravening creatures began fighting each other.

Borron now took the ship slowly towards the caves in which the Norroans had their homes – obviously, from their uniformity and regularity, artificial ones – with the evident intention of putting down the man they had rescued. This the old fellow must have realized, and from the fuss he kicked up he did not approve. What he said in his own language – if a series of clicks and rattles in his throat could be called a language – no one knew; but his actions were eloquent. It was clear that he wanted to go the other way.

'What do you suppose this is all about?' the Professor asked Vargo.

'If we go in the direction towards which he is pointing we may find out,' replied Vargo.

Borron complied, still keeping low and taking the ship towards the trees.

It did not take them long to discover the reason for the old man's anxiety. Some of his companions had been 'treed' – in the tree, presumably, from which they had been picking fruit. Somewhat surprisingly their besiegers at the foot of the tree were not the dog-cats that had pursued the rest of the party. They were small, black, yellow-spotted animals, something like miniature leopards. But what they lacked in size they made up for in numbers. There must have been hundreds, spitting and snarling as they glared with baleful eyes at three men sitting on the topmost branch.

'Lucky for those chaps that the little darlings below can't climb trees,' observed Toby.

'Dear me! Dear me!' exclaimed the Professor. 'What a perfectly appalling place to live, for ever hunted by predatory animals. It would need more cartidges than you have brought with you, Group-Captain, to dispose of that horde. What can we do to help those poor fellows?'

Borron answered the question. It was perfectly simple. He lowered the ship to the top of the tree and the men, under the instructions of the Norroan already aboard, clambered in. Borron then took the ship to the mouth of the nearest cave, landed, and put them off. Their countrymen, who must have been watching from behind their log-barred doorways, came out with loud, uncouth cries of welcome. At least, Rex hoped they were cries of welcome, for the noise was alarming, and this the size and appearance of the strange star-dwellers did nothing to alleviate.

However, all went well. The Norroans showed no signs of gratitude for what their visitors had done. Their attitude seemed to indicate that such adventures were an everyday affair, and narrow escapes as much a part of their existence as they must be for creatures that live in holes on Earth. But then, the Norroans were a primitive people, not to be judged by Earthly standards of culture. That is not to say they were a 'missing link' type. They were definitely human beings, as were the people of Lin; and this clear dividing line between men and animals struck Rex as significant. It could not, he thought, be mere accident. It could only be the purpose of the Creator of all things.

The fruit that had been dropped was collected and brought in, the collectors keeping a watchful eye on the woods. The Professor chose some specimens. He also took measurements, and photographs, the people obviously having no idea of what he was doing. There were some queer-looking nuts in one of the baskets. Rex found them impossible to break. A smiling boy cracked one for him with a finger and thumb. But Rex already knew from the effortless way the people handled the tree trunks that guarded their homes that their strength had not been exaggerated.

One surprising thing, considering the conditions in which they lived, was the absence of any sort of weapon beyond pointed sticks. If metals occurred in the ground either they had not been discovered or the people had not learned how to utilize them. They had not even invented the most common of all weapons – the bow and arrow. While the Professor was inspecting a cave dwelling Rex made one for them – to their great delight. It was not a powerful one, but it revealed the principle, and he hoped they would have the sense to develop it for use against the beasts which, although they did not appear to realize it, must have made their lives one long tribulation. Many of the men had frightful scars, clearly the result of encounters with the beasts; but there were no signs of sickness.

Perhaps the most astonishing thing was their ignorance of fire, although being vegetarians they would not need it for cooking purposes. They could manage without it. It was Tiger who pointed out the absence of smoke or ashes near the dwellings. To ascertain if they understood fire he lighted one, and the question was answered when they tried to pick it up, burning their fingers. Tiger showed them how to keep the fire burning by feeding it with sticks.

There was no cultivation. Apparently the Norroans were sufficiently well provided by nature.

The visitors stayed about two hours, not venturing far from the ship. The Professor took a sample of water for analysis at a later date, thinking it might throw light on the Norroans' uncommon physique and strength. Conversation being impossible nothing more could be learned, so when Vargo suggested they should be moving on no one demurred. They entered the ship to a barbaric chorus of howls. The doors were closed and the *Tavona* went on its way.

7 The little beasts of Kund

The inhabitants of Kund, their next port of call, were, stated Vargo, as unlike the people of Norro as it was possible to imagine. They were small. They were vicious. And they were cannibals, although this, he conceded, was not entirely their fault. They had to eat each other in order to live, because there was very little else, this being due in part to the nature of the planetoid and in part to overcrowding. Their skins varied in colour from blue-black to white, with many intermediate shades. In fact, their skins changed colour according to where they lived from time to time.

There was a reason for this, a reason as logical as sun tan on a white skin on Earth. The cause was the same.

In the first place the little planet had no orbit. By some curious freak of gravity it remained practically stationary in space. Secondly, it had ceased to revolve.

As the Professor presently pointed out, there was nothing unique about this. Mercury, the planet nearest the sun, did not revolve, always having the same face turned towards the sun. In the same way Earth's Moon always had the same side turned to its parent, Earth. Thus was it, apparently, with Kund. The result was, on the side facing the sun it was always light. The other side was always dark. There was a dividing zone of perpetual twilight. The side facing the sun was mostly desert and produced only an insignificant vegetation. The sunless side was not much better, being, naturally, extremely cold. The most productive area was the intermediate zone, for both animal and vegetable life.

The effect of these odd conditions was not really surprising.

They had produced two tribes, and these were always at war with each other, each tribe striving to gain control of the best – the intermediate – land. Sometimes one side had the advantage, sometimes the other. Always faced with starvation both sides ate their casualties and any prisoners they took – a state of affairs not unknown on Earth.

The people on the dark side of this unhappy world had pale skins, although on their raids into the sunny side they quickly became dark. Conversely, should the dark skins venture into the sunless side their skin at once began to lose its pigmentation.

How long this fantastic state of things had been going on Vargo did not know. From the accounts of early Lentoan and Minoan voyagers it had been so in their day.

'In which case they must have nearly exterminated themselves,' averred the Professor.

'On the contrary,' declared Vargo. Nature, always striving for a balance, he explained, had caused them, with a birthrate unknown elsewhere, to multiply, so that they became more instead of fewer. Thus, the conditions that had brought about the war had been aggravated, and what at first had been merely an inter-tribal war had become a desperate battle for survival.

'What will they do to us if we land?' asked Rex anxiously.

'Curiously enough, no ship landing there has ever been involved in serious trouble,' replied Vargo. 'They look forward to such visits because it has been the custom of visitors to barter foodstuffs, and other things useful to them, for a very beautiful green crystal which must occur in large quantities because, it being hard, they tip their spears with it.'

'On Earth,' said the Professor pensively, 'there was once a famous explorer named Captain Cook who often called at cannibal isles. For a long time he was made welcome because he carried food and other useful things: but one day they turned on him and he was killed and eaten.'

'I wouldn't trust these people of Kund too far myself,' admitted Vargo. 'Perhaps you would rather we did not stop there?'

'No – no. I didn't mean that,' protested the Professor. 'Sooner or later spaceships from Earth will explore the Solar System, so the guidebook I propose to write should be as complete as possible – like the Admiralty Sailing Directions for ships on the oceans of Earth.'

Rex did not say so, but he couldn't help feeling that the Professor's determination to make his manual complete was more likely to result in it never being written at all. But still, he reflected, the work would have to be done by someone, one day. Had the early navigators not been prepared to take chances the map of Earth would still be incomplete. The truth was, he suspected, the wide variations in the peoples they had seen in their travels was upsetting the Professor's theory that originally they had all sprung from a common race, either within the Solar System or beyond it. 'What about the atmosphere?' he asked Vargo.

Vargo said it was bad, containing a high percentage of helium; but it would be possible to tolerate it for a little while without spacesuits. Their suits would be more comfortable, but if they wore them the difficulties of communication would arise.

In view of Vargo's disturbing revelations it was with some trepidation that Rex regarded the war-torn world of Kund when, after a long run in which everyone had a meal and some sleep, it came into view. The angle of approach was such that even from a distance it was possible to see the two halves, the light and the dark. Borron said he would land on the light side, which would be warmer than the other, but before doing so he would run a little way down the intermediate area to see if there was anything of interest. It was there, he thought, that people were most likely to be seen.

69

The general panorama was a dreary picture. What Vargo had said about the lack of vegetation was true. Most of the surface of the globe presented to the visitors appeared to be desert. In other respects, too, Vargo's allegations were confirmed. Skirmishes were going on in several places. One was large enough to be called a battle. Not that there was any order about it. The light skins and the dark skins were in a general mix-up, chasing each other or hammering at each other with clubs, in the style of every man for himself. Quite a few were stretched out on the ground – ready for the table, as Toby put it.

'Well, there they are, still at it,' said Vargo. 'Do you still want to land?'

'Yes, but not in the battle,' returned the Professor. 'There's obviously not much to see, but I'd like a close view of these belligerent fools. In particular I'd like to examine their skins, for colour and texture.'

Borron, at Vargo's request, moved the ship farther into the light area and allowed it to settle gently on a bed of gravel near a ravine, on the edge of which stood a group of small, squalid huts. His idea, presumably, was to grant the Professor his wish to see natives at close quarters without the risk of becoming involved in the non-stop war. Certainly it seemed as safe a place to land as anywhere, for had there been many people there they could hardly have failed to show themselves.

It so happened that there was nobody there at all, as the visitors learned when, without putting on their spacesuits – for they did not intend to stay – they walked the thirty paces or so from the ship to the village. To be precise, the visiting party consisted of the Professor, Toby, and Rex, Tiger contenting himself by sitting on the step to watch, and, as he said, have a smoke. None could have suspected what this casual arrangement was to mean to the whole party.

Approaching the houses the investigators were greeted by

an abominable smell. The reason was not far to seek, for bones, looking like monkey bones, lay strewn about all over the place. Actually, the aroma was more of an animal smell than a human one, and it instantly brought back to Rex memories of the zoo. A heap of smouldering wood ashes suggested a recent feast, but no one commented on it.

The Professor, who was leading, stopped and hailed. There was no answer. 'No one at home,' he said, in a disappointed voice, and walked on slowly towards the doorway of the nearest house. Rex, having no wish to enter, for the smell outside was bad enough, strolled on towards the edge of the ravine, intending to see if it held anything of interest. He never reached it.

Over the brink, without the slightest warning, hooting like owls, poured a swarm of miniature human beings of such bestial appearance that Rex turned and fled incontinently towards the ship. It was their size that shook him as much as anything. Not more than three feet tall they looked more like animals than men. They had practically no foreheads; their noses were broad and flat and their mouths enormous. Their skins were pale in colour, so even in his panic Rex realized they must have come from the dark side of the globe, possibly having made their way into enemy country along the bottom of the ravine in order to raid the village. He did not get far. Something struck him between the shoulder blades and knocked him flat on his face.

The rest was sheer nightmare. Gasping, for the breath had been knocked out of him, he scrambled to his feet only to be knocked down again by the surging mob. Getting up again, not knowing whether he was on his head or his heels, as the saying is, he became aware that Toby was standing over him, yelling, and swinging a weapon of some sort.

There was a crashing report, and in a dazed sort of way Rex realized that Tiger was taking a hand; and to good purpose, for at the gunshot the uproar ceased as abruptly as a radio switched off. For two or three seconds the savages stood as if stricken with paralysis, and the short respite gave Rex and Toby a chance to reach the door of the ship, on the step of which Tiger was standing with the rifle in his hands. With a shout he fired again, shooting over the heads of the natives, and that was enough to put them to flight. But by this time the Professor had run out of the house, and, of course, met the crowd going the other way. In an instant he was knocked off his feet. Yelling, he was picked up, and in another moment had been carried out of sight over the lip of the ravine.

Everyone outside the ship raced for the spot. Rex found himself gazing into a chasm so deep that he recoiled with a cry of dismay. The sides were steep but not precipitous, and ended at a lake from which the people of the village no doubt got their water, as a narrow path, cut in the nearer bank, descended to it. Down this path, held by his arms and legs, the Professor was being carried by his captors. Tiger tore after them, shouting. Compared with the natives he looked enormous, and to them must have appeared a terrifying figure, a giant. Anyway, they fled in such haste that they dropped their prisoner, and crowding each other forced some of their number off the path so that they went bumping and rolling down the steep bank.

When the rescue party reached the Professor he was sitting on the ground looking more than somewhat dishevelled. 'Please take care not to step on my glasses,' he pleaded. 'Those little ruffians knocked them off. Dear me. I really began to think I was going to end my career in a stew pot.'

They helped him up, and making their way slowly to the top, came upon the lost glasses, fortunately not broken.

'Quite an alarming little business,' observed the Professor as he put them on. 'But then,' he added, 'if we go poking about other people's property we must expect a little trouble sometimes.'

As they reached the top, cries from below made them turn and look down. The natives were coming back, and the reason was plain to see. In hot pursuit was a large party of blue-skins who had presumably struck the enemy trail and followed it.

'I think it would be a good idea if we moved on,' remarked Tiger. 'There's going to be a rough-house here presently and if we get caught in it we may still end up on a spit over the fire.'

'I agree,' returned the Professor. 'Certainly this is no place for a picnic. Indeed, if we stay we may find ourselves the meat in the sandwich, as the doctor would say. You can bring one of these spears along, Rex, for a souvenir,' he concluded, indicating a number of weapons that had been dropped in the mêlée.

Rex picked one up. It was a crude instrument – a rough wooden handle to the end of which had been lashed a pointed slither of shining, green, glass-like substance. Reaching the top of the ravine they stopped to look back and saw a conflict raging too far below to cause them any anxiety. Before going on board the Professor took the weapon from Rex and examined the point closely.

He chuckled as he handed it back. 'One lesson we have learned is that values are local. I mean, things that are precious in one world can have no value on another. That, of course, is the result of supply and demand, and the uneven distribution of elemental materials throughout the universe. Here, for instance, having no other use for it, they can afford to tip their spears with precious stone – emerald, to be precise.'

'Emerald!' exclaimed Rex.

'Unless I am mistaken, yes. Emerald can occur in very

large lumps at home, but always being badly flawed it is hard to get even a small piece of clear, transparent crystal. These people, it seems, have a large supply of the stuff, and finding that it splits easily along the flaws have put it to practical use instead of using it as a sign of wealth, as is done on Earth. Well – well. We are learning quite a lot. But I hear sounds that suggest we should be well advised to go on board and remove ourselves from this abominable little planet. I think we have seen as much as we need of it.'

They all filed into the ship, which rose clear of the ground just as the first of the warring tribes appeared over the edge of the ravine, still fighting.

8 The Terror

The next planetoid on Borron's chart was, in his own language, named Stontum. They did not reach it. They never saw it. It was one of the larger bodies on the outer edge of the galaxy, the most distant from Mars, and the turning point from which the return journey would begin.

How far it was from Lentos in terms of Earthly miles, Rex, of course, had no idea, for such things as time and distance, in his own standard of measurement, had lost their meaning. In any case, the matter does not arise, because long before they were within sighting distance of the new objective the ship was involved in one of those holocausts which they knew could occur, and on their early voyages they had feared. Familiarity with space travel had lulled their apprehensions, and it was now, when the peril was almost forgotten that they met it head on, so to speak. Where the thing actually had its origin they did not know, except that it must have been in outer space, millions of miles away, or the whole Solar System must have been affected.

They became aware that something tremendous was happening, or had already happened, when the ship was filled with a blinding white light that grew and grew in intensity until it seemed to scorch the eyeballs. Rex closed his eyes and put his hands over them; yet so intense was the light that it penetrated his hands and eyelids and still reached his brain. What had happened he did not know, but he was sure this was the end for all of them.

The light grew brighter for perhaps two minutes, and at the peak persisted for several more; then, slowly, it began to fade – white to yellow, to orange, orange to red, red to purple and finally black.

Rex opened his eyes. Everything was dim, and fast becoming darker. 'What was it?' he managed to get out, in a thin voice. Actually, he was surprised to find the ship still intact.

'I would say a Nova,' answered the Professor. 'You may remember me speaking of them. They are often visible from Earth.'

'You mean – a star blew up?'

'Say, rather, destroyed itself by thermo-nuclear fission, probably as the result of a collision.'

As the ship did not appear to have been damaged Rex began to recover from his shock. 'How far away was it?' he asked.

'No one could answer that question,' returned the Professor. 'The explosion may have occurred long ago, but so far away that the light has only just reached us. The light from some of the distant stars, fast though it travels, may be hundreds of years reaching us. Even the light of the sun takes eight minutes to reach Earth, so that the sunrise you see actually occurred eight minutes earlier.'

Inside the ship it was now so dark that Rex could only just see the others.

'Where are the stars, anyway?' asked Tiger, who had joined Vargo and Borron at an observation window.

It must be remembered that, from the ship, stars were always visible, some large some small, all around. Usually there were several planetoids in sight, for the ship was in the thick of the belt that lies between Mars and Jupiter. Rex, looking out, could see none. All was black.

By this time Borron was giving orders in a tense voice. Pressure began to crush Rex in his seat and he knew that the progress of the ship had been accelerated to the limit of endurance. This lasted for several uncomfortable minutes. Then Borron rapped out another order. At once the pressure began to relax. A few minutes later Rex had to hold his seat to remain in it. No one spoke. What was happening Rex didn't know, but he was terribly afraid. Obviously something was wrong.

Fear dried his lips as the last faint light gave way to utter darkness. He could see nothing, inside the ship or out. He cried out involuntarily as something struck the ship with a vicious swishing noise and made it rock. It was the absolute darkness that made it so frightening. He knew it was no use asking for light because the ship carried no artificial lighting apparatus. There was no need for it. In the ordinary way it was always light because there was no night. Even when planetoids passed between them and the sun the brightness was only slightly dimmed. Why had the ship bumped? It could only mean that there was a force of some sort outside.

At last Vargo spoke. 'We have run into a zone of atmosphere caused by the explosion. With it came dust or frozen particles of gas. That is why it is dark. It will pass. How long that will take it is impossible to say. It depends on the volume of the zone.'

'But can't we get out of it?' cried Rex.

'Borron tried. You must have felt the pressure,' came Vargo's voice in the darkness. 'But he had to stop,' he went on. 'It was too dangerous to continue. Several planetoids must have been engulfed in this same cloud, so to proceed would be to invite collision with one of them.'

'Do you mean we've actually *stopped*?' asked Rex.

'Relatively speaking. By which I mean the energy has been cut. But we are still moving with the cloud – being carried along by it. That is why there is no longer any noise. Everything – gas, dust, and probably some lesser planetoids – are all moving in the same direction at the same speed.'

The Professor spoke. 'Obviously there can be no indication of how long these conditions are likely to persist,' he said. 'Too many are involved. Eventually I imagine, the dust will disperse sufficiently for us to see what we are doing, and that, surely must depend on the size of the cloud, which is an unknown quantity.'

'Always provided,' returned Vargo calmly, 'that the cloud is not dragged into the orbit of one of the larger bodies around us. Eventually, of course, that is bound to happen. The dust will fall somewhere. Let us hope that it thins sufficiently for us to get our bearings before that occurs.'

'The dust might fall on Earth,' suggested Rex.

'That would not be the first time the Earth and its satellite Moon have been showered with meteoric dust and gas,' asserted the Professor. 'The ancient records contained in the Old Testament of the Bible leave us in no doubt of that.'

'Let us hope,' said Vargo soberly, 'that when we emerge from this darkness Borron will be able to pick up his bearings, for it is by the stars and the planetoids around that he steers the ship. If they remain hidden, or if they should have moved, it would not be easy to find our way home. Our water and provisions will only last a certain time.'

'If we ran out we could always land somewhere and find some,' suggested Rex hopefully. 'The old mariners had to do that when they lost their way.'

'Having seen something of the worlds around us let us pray that will not be necessary,' said Toby drily.

But as things turned out, that is just what they were forced to do.

How long the ship remained in total darkness Rex did not know; but it was a long time, and before the end of it he felt he was in some danger of losing his reason. That was the real peril. Nothing could be done. The wisdom of Borron's decision to go with the cloud of dust was not to be disputed, although as the hours passed there were moments when he himself would have taken the risk of collision rather than endure the torture of uncertainty in the dreadful darkness. The only relief lay in conversation. They could not see each other, but it was something to be able to hear, and know the others were there. Borron told stories of the strange worlds he had visited. The others, in turn, talked of conditions on Earth. And so time passed. How far they had been carried off their course was not known, but it was thought to be a great distance, for the cloud, Vargo declared, without meeting any resistance, must be travelling at astronomical velocity.

The ordeal ended when Rex was asleep. He awoke to hear Tiger saying: 'Is it that my eyes are adapting themselves to the darkness or are the windows becoming grey – or at any rate, not so black as they were?'

There was a brief silence in which everyone must have been looking. Then Vargo said: 'They are grey. The dust is dispersing. Soon it should be light enough for us to see.'

And so it was. Little by little grey light crept in through the windows until, at long last, Rex could once more see his companions, although at first only vaguely. He nearly collapsed with relief, for the strain had been fearful. He felt he could bear anything as long as he could see.

Borron now improved matters by taking his ship slowly in the direction from which the light seemed to be coming. This had the desired effect, but they still moved through a world of gloom. Again Borron displayed his spacemanship, although Rex watched certain preparations among the crew without guessing what they were going to do. Two put on their suits, and taking a coil of line went into the airlock chamber. The inner door was closed, and a minute later the purpose of the operation was revealed when a ray of light pierced the ship and Rex saw a face looking in from outside. After his first start of alarm he realized that the men were cleaning the windows, the outer side of which had evidently picked up a coating of dirt. There was, of course, no risk of them falling. The rope was to enable them to move about.

This cleaning operation made a big difference and by the time the men had finished they could all see each other clearly. Conditions outside were not as bad as they had appeared from inside. That is not to say things were normal. Far from it. But with visibility improved it meant that Borron could increase the ship's velocity, all the time, of course, keeping a careful lookout. The light continued to improve, and after about an hour in Earthly time one or two of the brighter stars were peering mistily at them. This allowed Borron to make his first observations. But so long did he remain without speaking that the Professor asked him if he knew where he was.

'No,' answered Borron frankly.

'That's what I thought,' murmured the Professor.

'Such constellations as he can see are not in their usual places,' explained Vargo. 'But presently we may pick up a landmark.'

In the event they did not, and after a while Borron had to admit that he was completely lost. However, that did not mean they would never find their way back to Mino, although that might be difficult and take time. It was not so much the shortage of food and water that worried him as the exhaustion of the air supply. Should that happen it would, of course, mean the end.

Rex did not think about this. He could see, and that was enough to go on with. From the window he could see stars, with smaller ones appearing; but this was only in one direction. From the other side of the ship the sky was still unbroken black, the stars being hidden by the great cloudbank now moving away from them.

Borron now opened up to full velocity, with the object, as

he said, of making a wide circuit in the hope of picking up a planetoid, or better still, a group of them, that he could recognize. Identification of any one would give him his position.

After some time had elapsed they saw reflected sunlight catching one side of a very small planetoid and made their way towards it. It could not have been more than ten miles in diameter. As for the sun itself, which had at first revealed its position beyond the murk as a great brown globe, it now slowly turned to blue, sometimes dark and sometimes pale according to the composition and density of the intervening matter, which Borron affirmed might have been plain dust or frozen gas of some sort. Going close to the planetoid they made it out to be an arid wilderness with no sign of life. Borron consulted the crew but none was able to identify it. There was no distinguishing feature and the globe was typical of many smaller ones.

They went on to another, somewhat larger, with similar result. It was mostly desert with outcrops of rock. The only vegetation was a dwarf form of cactus which Borron said was common on many of the planetoids. They did not land, but pursued their quest for something that could be recognized.

As the lonely little world dropped away behind them the Professor remarked: 'It may well be that some of these balls of dirt contain minerals which will be of great value to civilized planets when their own resources have been used up. One day they will be exploited, and probably become theatres of war for the nations laying claim to them.'

'What are the chances of finding a new element, an unknown metal, for instance?' asked Toby.

'Very remote, I would say,' replied the Professor.

'We found a new metal on Mars – orichalcum,' reminded Rex.

'That was not a new metal; it was a very old one that had

been lost,' contended the Professor. 'Certainly none is known on Earth today, but that is not to say there is none there. It was known in ancient Atlantis. There may be more somewhere, deep in the ground. An entirely new mineral would be a wonderful discovery.'

Borron was now making for a much larger planetoid on which the sun was shining. Actually it was in partial eclipse. Its diameter might have been a hundred miles. Rex hoped that there would be some inducement to land, for he was tired of sitting still and would have welcomed a chance to stretch his legs. So he watched the globe becoming larger as they approached with more than usual interest. It had at least one conspicuous feature; a large lake; just one. It looked like water, but Borron warned them that this was not necessarily the case. On some worlds there were lakes of oil, of bitumen, and similar substances. The disappointing thing about this particular lake was that Borron could not recall seeing it before. An elderly member of the crew, who had served in the Remote Survey Fleet, said it struck a chord in his memory but he would not swear to it. In any case, he did not know the position of the globe in relation to the regular space routes. There was some vegetation, including small, stiff-looking trees, so Borron said he would land and test the place for an atmosphere. Whether there was one or not it would do them good to have a little exercise, even if they had to wear spacesuits.

He chose one of the wide sandy areas that fringed the lake, and presently the *Tavona*'s legs scraped softly on the surface. Everyone sat still while Vargo made the usual test for atmospheric conditions. This was soon done, with results which while disappointing, were not unexpected. There was no air to speak of. A little hydrogen and carbon dioxide, that was all. Suits would have to be worn if they went out.

Rex was hoping they might find some fruit or vegetables,

and made a remark to that effect. But Vargo warned him sternly to eat nothing until it had been examined, for while fruits and berries were sometimes found in these out-of-the-way places as often as not they were poisonous. Even where natives ate the fruit with impunity it did not mean they were safe for strangers.

'Like the honey at Trebizond and some of the wheat in Siberia, which have been known to put visitors on their backs,' put in the Professor, as those who had decided to go out began putting on their spacesuits.

'Be careful, everyone,' cautioned Vargo, before he closed his headpiece. 'This place, like others, may not be as safe as it appears from inside the ship.'

9 World without a name

For what happened on the unnamed planetoid Rex was to blame. He knew it. And his behaviour was perhaps all the more difficult to understand because he had a premonition of danger from the moment he put foot on the yielding sand outside the ship. But it is easy to be critical after the event. The fact of the matter was, a preliminary survey revealed not the slightest sign of danger, and this probably induced a feeling of security which was not justified considering where he was and what he was doing. Experience should have taught him that on unexplored worlds the apparent absence of perils did not mean there was none.

For a little while they all stood together just outside the ship in order to get their balance, for not only was gravity slight but they were all feeling the effects of being shut up in the ship for a long time. That the lake was in fact water or a similar liquid was at once evident, and Vargo fetched a vessel with the intention of taking a sample for analysis to see if it was fit to drink, or what was just as important, safe to wash in. It did not look inviting. It was black in colour, and the absence of any vegetation near the edge helped to give it a sinister appearance. In actual size the lake might have been two miles long by half a mile wide. Only at one point, not far away, did some coarse scrub approach nearer than a hundred yards. For the rest, the shore was a flat sandy beach, without a rock or even a stone.

While the others' backs were turned Rex thought he detected a slight ripple at one spot, and commented on it. The Professor said he must be mistaken, because with so slight an atmosphere there could hardly be any wind. Rex said there might be fish in the water, but the Professor brushed the idea aside saying it was most unlikely. For this casual dismissal of Rex's observation he was later to accept responsibility. Then, Vargo and the Professor walked towards the water while the others did as they wished. Alert for danger Rex strolled a little way along the beach, but seeing nothing of interest turned half right towards the nearest clump of trees to see if they bore fruit. He was not optimistic, for the trees did not look the sort that would bear fruit. They were dwarf but sturdy, with branches standing out stiffly almost from ground level. The foliage was dark bluish-green in colour. From a distance the leaves looked small and spiny, like broad pine needles. Between the trees and all around them flourished a coarse kind of grass with open patches of sand, and here and there a clump of scrub of the cactus family.

As he drew near he saw to his delight that the trees did in fact bear fruit in the shape of a small blue pineapple. It was this, he perceived, that from a distance had given the foliage its blue tint. He decided to gather some and take it to the ship to see if Borron or any of the crew could identify it. Advancing somewhat incautiously with this purpose in view he put a foot in a hole and nearly fell. Recovering, and looking about him, he saw holes all around, rather in the manner of a rabbit warren except that the holes were larger. From the heaps of sand outside the holes it was clear that they were not a natural formation, but must have been made by a creature of some sort. It was, of course, at this point that he should have turned back. The thought did not even occur to him. Meditating subconsciously perhaps in terms of rabbits and being anxious to reach the fruit he took another pace or two forward. Then he came to a dead stop. For good reason.

A little way in front, near a clump of scrub, almost level with the ground, two green eyes were watching him. At first he could see nothing else, for the body of the creature was practically the same colour as the ground. A more repulsive beast he had never seen. It was, he perceived, a reptile, in size about four feet long. Its mouth was slightly open, revealing two rows of sharp, wicked-looking teeth. The brute recalled to Rex's mind pictures he had seen of the hideous monitor lizards that live on the Galapagos Islands in the Pacific.

Now Rex was more disgusted than afraid. Certainly the creature was ugly, but it was not very large and he did not suppose for a moment that it would attack him. He also imagined that its movements would be slow and clumsy. He was sharply disillusioned when without warning the beast shot forward as if impelled by a spring. It came open-mouthed with its back arched, its carapace looking like a row of knives. Rex leapt aside, narrowly escaping the teeth. In doing so he put his foot in another hole and nearly came down. But he managed to keep his feet, and again had to leap as the brute, which had skidded to a stop, came back at him. A second lizard now appeared, and to his horror he saw others emerging from their holes. Some were behind him, so seeing his retreat cut off he took the only course open to him, which was up the nearest tree. Although there were plenty of branches, in his spacesuit this was no easy matter, for he had to force his way between them, well aware that should he tear the fabric his end would be swift. He could hear teeth snapping below him, and for a ghastly moment thought the lizards were able to climb trees, too. Luckily this was not the case, as he observed when, getting astride a branch at the top of the tree he looked down. Even so, the picture presented was bad enough. There were now about twenty of the creatures there, all staring up at him.

He called for help over his radio, and there must have been something in his voice to bring Tiger and Toby towards the spot at the fastest speeds possible in their clumsy gear. Then realizing that they were unarmed Rex yelled at them to keep away. 'Bring the rifle – the rifle,' he shouted, by no means sure that one rifle would be enough to deal with the pack of monsters gaping at him. Tiger went back, but Toby came on slowly, looking for the cause of Rex's predicament, which from his position he could not see. Rex shouted to him to stay where he was. Tiger reappeared with the rifle. Vargo and the Professor, some distance farther way, began walking up the beach.

Events now took a turn beyond imagination. It was a shout from the Professor that called attention to them. Both he and Vargo broke into a run and the reason did not take Rex – still perched in his tree – long to find. From the water were emerging the creatures which presumably had caused the ripples. They were snakes, or eels, Rex was not sure which. They were quite small, but they came in such unbelievable numbers that it looked as if a black shadow was spreading up the beach. They made no attempt to pursue the two men hurrying away from them. It was apparently their feeding time, for they made for the nearest area of grass, this, presumably, being the stuff on which they lived. At all events, there appeared to be nothing else there.

The most fantastic feature of the whole business now occurred, and as before, it could not have been anticipated. If the eels lived on the grass then it seemed that the lizards lived on eels, for the instant they were seen Rex was abandoned as the whole pack tore pellmell into the thick of the squirming serpents.

Then came such a spectacle as Rex had never expected to see and never wanted to see again. The eels, or watersnakes, made no attempt to defend themselves; nor did they endeavour to reach the water. They went on feeding, even though their nearest neighbours were scooped up by the lizards and swallowed whole. More eels came out of the water farther along. More lizards rushed down and tore into them. Rex found it hard to believe that this disgusting business was really happening. Not that he wasted much time looking at it. Seeing that the ground below was clear he hastened down and made for the ship with all the speed he could manage. The others were standing by, waiting, Tiger a little in advance of the others, and it was upon this trifling detail that Rex's life probably depended.

He was still some yards away when he became aware that something was wrong. His suit was becoming soggy and he felt that his body was swelling – as indeed it was. With failing sight he fought for breath, and even as darkness closed in on him he knew that he must have punctured his suit, allowing the air, and consequently the pressure, to escape.

When he came round he was lying on the floor of the ship. The doors were closed and the others were around him, Toby kneeling. His suit was half on and half off. For a few seconds, as is usual when one recovers from unconsciousness, he couldn't make out where he was or what was happening.

'All right. Lie still. Take it easy,' said Tiger.

Rex complied. He was in no state to argue. And as he lay there, his senses returning to normal, he remembered everything. 'I must have torn my suit in the tree, going up or coming down,' he said weakly.

'Had you torn it going up it's hardly likely you would be here now, my boy,' asserted Toby. 'You would have dropped off the tree like an over-ripe apple, straight into the mouths of those ugly devils watching you. You must have pricked it coming down. Luckily it was only a small puncture or nothing could have saved you. By the time we had got you into the pressurized cabin you had so swollen into your suit that we could hardly get at you. Feeling all right now?'

'A bit giddy, that's all,' answered Rex. 'My eyes are a bit blurry.'

'I don't wonder. Another minute and they'd have popped out. Don't worry. They'll soon adjust themselves.'

The Professor stepped in, speaking seriously. 'In moments of excitement it is easy to forget that in airless conditions one is entirely dependent on one's clothing. Without air, and the artificial pressure it provides, swift death is inevitable. Let no one forget that.'

After his narrow escape Rex was sure he never would forget it.

'Let us move off,' Vargo,' said the Professor. 'No useful purpose is to be served by staying here any longer.'

The crew took their places at the controls. Borron gave his usual orders. The ship quivered, otherwise it did not move. Another order and the quiver stopped. The crew looked at each other. 'Something seems to be wrong,' said Vargo. He went to the window and looked out. 'The legs have sunk into the sand,' he explained, calmly. 'The floor is almost level with the ground.'

'But haven't we enough power to pull the ship out of the ground?' asked the Professor, in the silence that followed Vargo's statement.

'We have no power at all,' returned Vargo. 'The exhaust ends of the energy tubes are blocked by the sand.'

'If you turn on full power it might blow them clear,' suggested Tiger.

'With no exhaust outlets it might blow the ship to pieces,' said Vargo simply.

As in other dangerous situations Rex noticed that the crew showed no signs of fear.

'What's to be done?' inquired the Professor.

'Some of us will have to go out and dig the power tubes clear of sand,' said Vargo. 'It's the only way. And we had better make haste or it will be impossible. If, as it seems, we are in quicksand, the ship will be sinking deeper every minute.'

At the idea of being trapped on this beastly place once more Rex's stomach seemed to go down like a lift. Not that it mattered much where they ended up if they could never get back to Earth. He got to his feet as some of the others went into the airlock chamber, but realizing that with a damaged suit he could not go out he took it off, whereupon one of the crew took it from him and set about repairing it with equipment carried for the purpose. He could hear scraping going on under the ship and from time to time it shook slightly as if attempts were being made to lift it.

It seemed a long time before Borron came in and went to the controls. He applied the energy, and Rex, to his unspeakable relief, felt the ship move. Outside, clouds of sand swirled, showing that the tubes were clear. Then the inner door of the airlock opened and those who had gone out came in.

A moment later, through his window, Rex saw the horizon begin to fall away, and knew that the *Tavona* had resumed its flight. That, at least, was something to be thankful for, he told himself; but they were still lost in the great open spaces of the Solar System. At least, he could only hope that they were still in their own group of planets, for had they got outside it, it was unlikely that they would ever see Mino, much less Earth again.

10 Strange sanctuary

It is hardly surprising that by this time Rex's enthusiasm for space exploration had declined considerably. All he wanted now was to get home, or at any rate back to Mino with its simple civilization; or better still, to Earth's next-door neighbour, Mars, which would almost seem like home. None of the worlds he had seen in his travels were to be compared with them.

The explorers, he thought, now knew what they had set out to discover. Most of the planetoids of any size had developed life in one form or another, usually unpleasant and always different; which suggested that the theory assigning all life to a common stock was wrong, and its alternative, which was that every world had produced life suitable to its conditions, was right. Just as they themselves would find it hard, if not impossible, to keep alive on most of these bodies, so any form of life they had seen, removed from its home, would probably die. They had all the evidence they needed, and the Professor could now spend the rest of his life working out why men on one planet should be giants, and on another, pygmies. It was a strange thought that should he find the answer it might be within his power to produce giants and dwarfs on Earth.

But before he could do that they would have to get there, and with their air supply and provisions shrinking daily their chances of succeeding in this were far from bright.

Vargo and Borron spent most of their time studying the stars; and it might be thought that as they were familiar with them they would have no difficulty in fixing the position of the ship. Actually, as Vargo explained, it was their own position that prevented this. They were in the middle of the vast system of planetoids, some thousands of which had been observed, and given names or numbers, by astronomers on Earth. It was now known that the total number was far greater. They were not fixed stars. Every one, in the inexorable grip of gravity, had its own particular orbit, sometimes large, sometimes small. Some planetoids moved swiftly, some slowly. Some were near to them, others far away. Then again, whether it moved under its own power or was impelled by gravity, the ship itself was moving through space at astronomical speed.

These factors made it almost impossible to recognize any particular star, or constellation of stars, from a distance, for reasons which are easily explained. From hour to hour all the host of bodies around the ship varied in magnitude – the scale used to determine the size and distance of a star by its brilliance. Thus, a small planetoid near the ship, in the full glare of the sun, might for a period appear to be a star of the first magnitude, only to diminish to a star of lesser magnitude as it proceeded on its orbit. Again, the brilliance of a planetoid could depend on its composition. They had seen how Unkos had blazed out of all proportion to its size because it had been fused by heat to a mass of glass, and glass is a reflector. The same with Pallio, with its glittering icy surface.

Borron admitted frankly that short of dropping by accident on a globe that he was able to recognize, the only chance of fixing the ship's position was to get clear of the planetoids altogether and so obtain an uninterrupted view of the well known Outer Stars. The trouble about that was the time it might take, not knowing from whence he was starting. He had no idea of how far the blast of the exploding Nova had carried them. As far as recognition was concerned, he and his crew knew a great many of the planetoids by sight, provided they were close enough to see the physical features; but there were more that they had never seen. Like mariners on the oceans of the Earth their travels had been confined to regular routes, and once off the beaten track, so to speak, everything was new and strange. The Nova had thrown them off their course and they were now in an unknown sea of space.

Vargo said the danger of getting off course had always been recognized. More than one ship of the Remote Survey Fleet had failed to return to base and this was thought to be the reason, although there was always a chance of a ship being struck by a meteor. They knew this had happened on at least one occasion, for the ship had been found floating in space with a large hole right through it. The crew, who had not been wearing their spacesuits at the time of the accident, having no time to put them on must have died instantly. The ship had been towed home.

It was cold comfort that Borron himself had never before been lost. However, as neither regrets nor complaints would help matters the atmosphere in the ship remained the same as it sped on its way seeking a way out of the difficulty. It seemed to Rex that their position might well be likened to that of a sailing ship that had been blown off its course by a gale. There were islands in the oceans of water, and there were also islands in the sea of space. The trouble was, there were too many of them. Several were surveyed during the next few days, but as they all turned out to be barren and airless no landings were made.

They had one remarkable experience during this period, and it astonished Vargo and Borron no less than the Professor, who said he had never considered such a possibility. The temperature inside the ship suddenly increased, and Borron announced that it could only be due to skin friction on the outside. That meant they were passing through a belt of atmosphere of some sort, although there was nothing to be seen outside to confirm this. The chances were, he thought, that it was most likely to be helium, argon, or carbon dioxide, as these were occasionally encountered. At the Professor's request he went into the airlock chamber to settle the question. He returned with a faint smile on his face to say that the atmosphere was a mixture with such a large proportion of oxygen that although it was thin, it was possible to breathe it. Unfortunately the pressure inside the ship was such as to prevent any from entering if he opened a valve.

That such a phenomenon could exist gave them something to talk about, and it was generally agreed that it was another result of the Nova explosion. Some unlucky planetoid had lost its atmosphere in the blast, and sooner or later another would capture it.

'So now we know why some planets have air and others haven't,' remarked Rex.

The Professor conceded that that seemed to be the answer.

But strange though this incident was it was soon to be forgotten in one more in the nature of a real old-fashioned adventure. It was one of those odd coincidences that it should happen so soon after Vargo had mentioned something of the sort.

The ship had for some time been heading for a star which at first, because it was dull, was thought to be small; but as they drew near they could see they had been mistaken. It was one of the largest they had seen. The dull reflection, declared Vargo, could only be the result of a cloak of vegetation or a thick belt of atmosphere. It turned out to be both. There was even some slight cloud. There were several lakes and a watercourse connecting two of them. From even closer inspection the vegetation appeared, from its smoothness, to be grass or reeds. With these promises of comfortable conditions the ship dropped towards it, Borron admitting with reluctance that he had no recollection of having seen the place before.

The ship was still at about a thousand feet, its power in reverse to check the fall, when a cloud of white smoke suddenly billowed upwards from some open ground near one of the lakes.

'Be careful, Borron,' warned Tiger. 'That looks like a volcano.'

'No,' disputed the Professor. 'The smoke from the crater of a volcano would be constant. That which we can see has only just appeared. It looks to me as if a fire has just been lighted.'

Nothing more was said. Everyone watched with mounting interest, for if a fire had been lighted it could only mean that there were people there. Moreover, there was reason to suppose that they were making a signal.

That this was in fact the case became evident when from a lower altitude it became possible to see figures round the fire, dancing and waving. They appeared to be as normal as themselves. Borron, however, was taking no chances, and held the ship off while he had a good look at them.

It was Toby who settled all doubts. 'Great Scott!' he cried. 'Isn't that a Flying Saucer over there, by the trees?'

'It is,' declared Tiger. 'It seems to be half on its side. Those trees have had some knocking about, too. Some have been snapped off short. It looks to me as if the place might have been hit by a thundering good storm.'

Borron, who, as usual, seemed to be unaffected by surprise or shock, put the ship down close to the fire. The men, there were eight of them, at once ran to it. Their clothes were in rags, but tall and fair they looked very much like Minoans. But the most important thing about them, from Rex's point of view, was that they wore no spacesuits. This meant quite definitely that the atmosphere was 'pure'.

'Castaways for certain, by all that's wonderful,' cried Tiger.

'A slice of cake for them we came along,' said Toby, grinning.

'It might turn out to be a slice of cake for us as well – if they know where they are,' returned Tiger.

Borron made a quick test of the atmosphere, although the pressure valve made the unusual recording that the air pressure outside the ship was greater than inside, and went out. The others followed in turn to find him in the centre of an excited little crowd and a babble of conversation. Rex knew not one word of the language being used, so he began to wonder who the strangers were. As physical specimens they were magnificent, perfectly proportioned and rather more heavily built than Lentoans or Minoans. His curiosity had to be restrained for some time, until Vargo was able to break away and tell them what it was all about. In the meantime he looked about him, mopping perspiration from his face for the air was sultry, both hot and humid, although why this should be was not apparent. From the number of broken trees that lay about it was plain that there had been a storm of wind of great violence. Even now Rex occasionally felt a slight breeze on his cheek – something he had not experienced for a long time. He also saw some winged insects, including a tiny blue butterfly that looked remarkably like the common Summer Blue of Earth. He had another shock when he noticed some thistles, and a straight row of shrubs, obviously cultivated, bearing what appeared to be large tomatoes. Taking one thing with another it was evident that conditions on this unknown little world resembled those of Earth more closely than any others they had seen. This gave the visitors from Earth something to talk about until Vargo was able to tell them the story of the castaways. And an amazing tale it was he had to tell. This was the gist of it.

How long the men had been marooned was not easy to explain, for there was no appropriate measurement of time, but as Rex made it out it was a matter of years.

The Spacemen, as Rex had suspected, were not Lentoans

or Minoans, but came from a wonderful world of great age, called by them Ando, far, far away. Rex was to get an idea of how far way when Vargo went on to explain that it was from this world that many people got their ships, the journey from Lentos to get one occupying more than a Lentoan sun-cycle of time.

These people, declared Vargo, were a very old civilization indeed, and had been building spaceships for so long that their origin was lost in the dim past. The Andoans were highly skilled in space travel, making voyages beyond belief. They knew the Solar System intimately, had surveyed every planet in it, and knowing the danger of interference with the natural order of things kept watch on scientific development. It was, in fact, to study the increasing number of explosions on Earth that this particular crew had been assigned. There was nothing to fear from that, for the Andoans were men of peace. This particular ship had reckoned to be away for a time equal to two years.

The trouble had occurred on the return journey when they had nearly collided with the planetoid which on Earth had been named Hermes. It had, they alleged, for no apparent reason extended the ellipse of its orbit, and in so doing may have interfered with other bodies. The result, it was thought, was the production of a small comet, previously unknown and therefore uncharted. They had seen it afar off, and, of course, had taken steps to avoid it; but it must have been travelling at tremendous velocity, casting stones from its tail over a wide area, and some of these had struck the ship.

The Captain, on sighting the comet, and realizing there might be some danger from it, had given orders for space-suits to be put on, and it was due to this precaution that there were any survivors.

Several red-hot stones had struck the ship and gone right through it, smashing instruments and killing three men, the

Captain and two of the crew. The second in command, who was also the navigator, had made for the nearest place known to him where atmospheric conditions made life possible in the hope of being able to put the ship in a state of repair sufficient for it to return to its distant base. It would be impossible to do this if they were compelled to wear spacesuits all the time, and obviously they would not be able to take them off in a ship in which there was neither air nor pressure. To repair the ship turned out to be a long and difficult business, and they were still at work on it when another disaster overtook them. The little planet was struck by a mass of air; or it might be more correct to say that it picked up a belt of loose air and held it by gravitational attraction. Either way the results were the same, the wind defying description. The visitors could see for themselves the damage that had been done by what was in effect, a tornado. The ship had been bowled over the ground by the blast into the position in which they now saw it, and was beyond repair. Two more men had been killed and others injured.

'Could that have been the belt of air we struck?' put in Rex.

'Possibly. Or part of it – what was left of it,' replied Vargo. 'Certainly not all of it because the disaster here occurred some time ago and much of the air was retained. That we know, for our friends here say that since the tornado the density of the air has been greater than before. Of even more interest, although such things have happened before to our certain knowledge, is their report that the storm brought certain visitors, some to their advantage, others not so good.'

'Visitors?' queried the Professor. 'What sort of visitors?'

'Insect and vegetable, probably carried in the form of eggs and seeds, from another world.'

The Professor nodded thoughtfully. 'There is no direct evidence, but there are some scientists who believe that such a thing may have happened on Earth. How very interesting.'

'That is one of the new vegetables,' stated Vargo, pointing at the thistles. 'When our Andoan friends first landed here there was none. They are now increasing so fast that they threaten to occupy the entire planet. The small blue butterflies you see were not here, either. Now their caterpillars are on everything. The plague is spreading fast, so that in the end they may denude the planet of its vegetation. The new air also brought a tiny biting insect which causes irritation and brings on fever. Thus can these space storms over a great period of time change the character of a planet, turning fertile lands to deserts, and deserts into gardens.'

'Insect and vegetable life could be carried from one planet to another in spaceships,' averred Rex, pointing to the open door of their own ship.

The Professor patted Rex on the shoulder. 'Excellent,' he congratulated. 'That certainly could happen. Aeroplanes on Earth are doing the very same thing.'

It was agreed that the Andoans had little cause for complaint in their choice of landing ground, for while the food supply was meagre by Earthly standards, consisting chiefly of fruit, roots, berries and grass seeds, they had no enemies to contend with.

'The point is, do they know where we are?' Tiger asked Vargo.

Vargo delighted them by saying yes, they did. They were on one of the most distant planetoids and therefore a long way from Mino.

'Can you tell me why it is so warm here at such a distance from the sun?' questioned the Professor. 'I would have expected to be frozen.'

'Quite easily,' answered Vargo, and went on to explain. The little planet they were on, like the planetoid Adonis, had an extremely elliptical orbit that took it, at one extremity, nearer to the Sun than Earth, actually passing between Earth and Venus. During its proximity to the Sun the heat was so intense that it was necessary to retire into the shade. But during that period the ground and its thick belt of dense atmosphere were charged with so much heat that it was not entirely lost at the cold end of the orbit. This was only made possible by the short period in which the orbit was completed, the journey taking a shorter time than any other known. The quick extremes of heat and cold were, of course, very trying, but could be endured. All forms of life on the planet had, as would be expected, adapted themselves to it. The rapid growth of the vegetation as the planet approached the sun was phenomenal. Vargo smiled. 'On the first trip round the Sun the Andoans feared everything would be burnt to a cinder.'

'Which way are we going now?' asked Rex.

'Towards the sun.'

'Which means that it will get hotter every day.'

'Naturally.'

'Then the sooner we get away the better.'

'By no means. We are already being carried nearer home every second.'

'Riding on an orbit,' chuckled the Professor, popping a caramel into his mouth.

'As I understand it,' put in Tiger, filling his pipe, 'we have only to sit still to pass near our real home, Earth.'

'And close to Mars on the way,' observed Toby. 'As Vargo says, it's more comfortable here than in the ship so we might as well sit still. What about our new friends, though? How are they going to get home?'

'They will come back with us to Mino,' said Vargo. 'Afterwards, one of their ships, or one of ours, will take them to their own world.'

'Good!' exclaimed the Professor. 'What fun this space travel is. I suggest we have something to eat. Some fresh tomatoes will make a nice change in our rather monotonous diet.'

11 Stars in their courses

Rex had no means of working out the passing of time, by Earthly standards, on their island in space which, by reason of its pleasant conditions, they had decided to name Arcadia; for not only was its orbit a fast one but its rate of revolution so high that day and night followed each other in swift succession. After the twenty-four-hour day in which he had spent most of his life Rex found this not a little bewildering. The day, the period when the side of the globe they were on was turned towards the Sun, was only about five hours as he still reckoned time. There was a brief twilight and then it was dark, the dark hours corresponding to those of daylight. The nights were comfortably warm, the side which had been exposed to the Sun retaining much of its heat through the short hours of darkness. Every day, as the planetoid approached its summer season, it became progressively warmer, until they were soon forced to seek shade during the glare of noon.

For the rest, so little sensation was there of being on a star, and so like were the conditions to the subtropical zones on Earth, that it often came as a shock to Rex to remember where he was. But, after all, there was nothing remarkable about that. Few people on Earth pause during their activities to remind themselves that they are on one of a million globes, spinning as they whirl through the limitless spaces of the Universe.

With the mounting temperature the vegetation became more and more tropical in its luxuriance, and had it not been for the tiny irritating flies Arcadia would have been as near perfection as Rex could have imagined. One and all agreed that Arcadia was far and away the most attractive world they had seen since leaving home.

This led to some discussion as to why a world so well adapted for human life had failed to produce any, particularly, as they had found human or sub-human populations on worlds less well-endowed. The same argument could be applied to the absence of mammals, birds and fish. That warm-blooded creatures had not yet had time to develop did not seem to be a very convincing explanation.

'As the place has such a congenial climate why not put some people on it as it passes the nearest point to Earth,' suggested Toby, smiling 'Start a new colony, in fact. You'll always find people ready to emigrate.'

'A camping holiday on a new planet, as an advertisement, should produce plenty of schoolboys looking for a thrill,' put in Rex, grinning.

'Funny to think that when space travel really gets into its stride this place might become a holiday resort' said Tiger. 'Most places on Earth are overrun already. And properly cultivated quite a lot of food could be produced here against the time Earth begins to run short. Arcadia would make a capital colony for people looking for a slice of free land.'

'I doubt it,' interposed the Professor.

Tiger looked surprised. 'Why?'

'Life would be too easy. Haven't you noticed that men most often succeed where life is a struggle against adverse conditions? Hard work brings out the best in them. In the smiling South Sea Islands, where life is easy and food plentiful, no progress was ever made towards a higher civilization. It is fear and necessity that drives men on to do their utmost. On the languorous Pacific islands people spend most of their time singing and dancing, with intervals of doing nothing at all.'

'They'll probably be singing and dancing when your higher civilizations have blown themselves to smithereens with atom bombs,' declared Toby, grimly.

The Professor smiled wanly. 'Good for you, Doctor. You got in a shrewd one at me there. I hope you're wrong, but I fear you may be right. But before talking of making Arcadia a colony someone would have to check all the seasons to make sure the place is really safe. I have a good mind to stay here and do the full trip round the Sun. It would be a fascinating experience, and an instructive one. For instance, I would get a close view of that lonely little planet, Mercury.'

'You're not serious!' exclaimed Rex.

'Indeed I am,' answered the Professor. 'Vargo could take you home and pick me up later.'

'He might never find this particular world again – what then?' said Rex.

The Professor chuckled. 'As you say, my boy, what then? I could think of worse places to spend my declining years, provided I had a good telescope and a notebook.'

The subject was not pursued, and the Professor's startling project did not materialize. For a very good reason.

A certain amount of exploring had been done without the discovery of anything particularly noteworthy. Sometimes they had gone off together as a party, but as time went on without the slightest sign of danger appearing Rex had taken more and more to going off alone, sometimes on quite long walks. These had served a useful purpose, for he usually collected fruit on the way home. So far his only adventure had been an amusing one. One day a breeze got up and to his astonishment he saw what he took to be a snowstorm coming towards him. But it turned out to be a great cloud of thistle seeds picked up by the breeze, and he recalled what Vargo had said about the invading weeds overrunning the planet.

But a far more serious adventure was in store, one that

altered their ideas about the security of their temporary home. At the time it so happened both Mars and Earth were in sight, Earth easily recognizable by its single moon, so there was no longer any risk of Borron again getting off his course. He knew just where he was, and already there had been talk of departure.

Rex went off on one of his jaunts and this time he went farther than usual, and in a new direction, his objective being some low cliffs which he could see in the distance. These he reached, or nearly reached, without incident, and he was approaching what looked like a dry watercourse, when with an involuntary cry of alarm he came to a dead stop, his eyes on a dark face staring fixedly at him through the sparse branches of a shrub. It did not move. Nor did he. Indeed, the shock had made him incapable of movement. Then, as he recognized the thing for what it was his nerves relaxed. Fear gave way to amazement and he moved forward for a closer examination of his discovery, a discovery, he realized instantly, of profound importance.

The thing was a graven image. It had the body of a lion-like animal with a sad human face. The top of the head had been carved into a fair representation of a feathered hat, something in the style of a Red Indian bonnet. Feathers – where there were no birds! An animal – where there were no animals! And a human face where there were no human beings! For a minute Rex was completely flabbergasted by what all this implied. How wrong their assumptions had been!

The thing was obviously an idol. By whom it had been carved, and presumably worshipped, was a question for which he never expected to find an answer. One thing, however, was quite certain. If the planetoid had no human population now it must have had one at some period, for only human hands could have fashioned such a piece of sculpture. That the thing was of great age was made apparent by the way the stone had weathered, the base providing a foothold for moss and lichen.

Deep in thought, looking about him for more signs of occupation, he went on to the dry watercourse, again to come to an abrupt halt, staring at some marks clearly defined in the hard, slaty bottom of the lost river near his feet.

It was a line of tracks, footprints of a large bird, or lizard, he didn't know which. All he knew for certain was that the tracks were much too large to have been made by any creature on the planet at that time. He knelt down to examine them and found, as he had anticipated, that the tracks were in hard stone. They could only have been made, therefore, when the stone was soft. How long ago that had been he had not the remotest idea, of course. The river bed was, he confirmed, slate, and that to some extent explained the mystery. For under the Professor's instruction he now knew enough about geology to be aware that slate is a sedimentary rock. That is to say it had once been mud, or silt, deposited by water; over the years, by pressure and exposure, it had hardened to its present form.

The picture was now fairly plain. While the rock had been soft, ages before, some creature had walked down the drying river bed. Naturally, this interested him enormously, because it told him that conditions on the planet had not always been the same as they had found them. That was a piece of real news to take home to the Professor. But more was to come.

Following the tracks he came upon more tracks which, without the slightest doubt, were human footprints, and must have been made at about the same period as the others. This discovery shook him, because it answered the question that had puzzled them, why did not the planet carry a human population? Now he knew beyond all shadow of doubt that it had. What had become of it was another matter. He carried on, still following the tracks.

His next discovery was a fossilized fish, quite a large one, about three feet long. The outline had been clearly impressed in the rock, even to the scales; but there seemed to be something wrong with the fins. He wasted no time on it. The Professor would probably know all about it when he saw it, as he would, when he heard of these enlightening finds. They were, decided Rex, more unexpected than really remarkable. After all, these things were fairly common on Earth in similar rock formations.

He went on, now following in the footsteps of the man who had passed that way perhaps a million years earlier. That alone was a sobering thought. He was now close to the cliffs, which he thought were limestone. Surveying them, his eyes came to rest on the entrance to a cave. Its irregular outline told him that it was natural, not artificial; and that again was in order, because most limestone formations are honeycombed with caves. The footsteps left the river bed in a direct line for the opening. So that, mused Rex, was where the fellow had lived. Or was it the lair of some beast which he intended to attack? Perhaps he could find out. Excited, slightly overcome by this link with the prehistoric past, he moved forward, slowly, for he was also a little apprehensive of what he might find. Reaching the entrance he saw not one but several footprints, some large, some small. Lying about, bleached white by the sun, were many bones, none of them large, and none of them, as far as he could make out, human.

The question now was, should he go on, or should he go back to report? He was torn both ways. In the end, prudence, supported by the need of an adequate torch for such an undertaking, won. But before turning for home he advanced to the threshold of the cave and peered inside. The entrance being high – it was really a wide fissure – a fair amount of light filtered in, so that when his eyes became accustomed to the gloom he had a fading view for about twenty paces. There was little to see. More bones lay about. Apart from these there was only one definite object. It was on the ground, not far in. Dark brown in colour it looked as if it might have been a large length of rough timber, such as a piece of tree trunk.

Rex stared at it: and the more he stared the more convinced he became that it was nothing of the sort. Slowly a grim suspicion as to what it was crept over him, and he went forward to investigate.

As he had suspected it turned out to be the body of a man. Not a skeleton, but a body, as dry and shrivelled as a smoked fish. It lay at full length, one arm reaching forward, as if the man had fallen and died while making a desperate attempt to get farther into the cave. The corpse had obviously been there for a very long time. Why? Why had his friends left him lying there? Why was the body parched like an old piece of leather? It looked as if it might have been scorched by fire. Conditions on the planet must certainly have been different when the man had lost his life, reasoned Rex, for as things were at present a body would quickly decompose.

He lingered a moment longer, staring fearfully into the dark recesses of the cave; then he made his way out, and turning away from this drama of the past hurried back to the ship. He did not stop to collect fruit on the way.

The brief twilight was nearly over when he rejoined the others. They were sitting round a fire, lighted to discourage the midges, which at this hour became more active than at any other time. Seeing from his manner that something unusual had happened they looked at him questioningly. He did not keep them waiting, but forthwith gave an account of his discoveries. 'You remember that body in the Egyptian Room at the British Museum – an Arab who had died of thirst lying in a hole in the sand? It had become sun-dried. Well, this body looked just like that,' he concluded.

'So there *was* once a human population here,' remarked the

Professor pensively. 'I can't say I'm surprised. We are now confronted with an interesting field for speculation. What became of it?'

'Whatever it was must have happened a very long time ago or we should have found signs of occupation, and according to the Andoans there was none,' observed Vargo.

'We *know* it must have been a very long time ago,' returned the Professor. 'The sedimentary rock tells us that. Silt doesn't become stone in a few hours. Let us not forget that at the time men were here there were also large animals, birds or reptiles. They, too, have gone, leaving only their tracks to tell us they existed. One thing is certain; something must have dried the surface mud of the river bed very quickly or the tracks would have been erased by the weather.'

'Thinking about it, I believe those tracks were only recently exposed,' said Rex. 'They might have been under sand. There was a lot of sand about, some of it heaped up as if by the wind.'

'The big storm while the Andoans were here might have shifted the sand,' opined Toby.

'Of course, forms of life do disappear in the course of time, from causes natural or otherwise,' went on the Professor, looking at the others over his spectacles. 'Sometimes the reason can be conjectured, sometimes not. Hundreds of creatures, many of them monsters, have disappeared from Earth. Let us suppose that Rex has seen the footprints of a large bird. It would be a reasonable supposition, since the people who lived here must have known about feathers – as is proved by the idol. If we ask ourselves why did that bird disappear from Arcadia we might as well ask why did that giant bird, the Moa, disappear from Earth. Its bones are still found in New Zealand. In Madagascar the digging of its enormous eggs from the mud, for collectors and museums, still provides a livelihood for some of the natives. That mud will doubtless harden as time goes on, as it has hardened here. New Zealand and Madagascar are islands in seas of water. Arcadia is an island in a sea of space. Broadly speaking there is little difference, so it should not astonish us that a large bird once dwelt here.'

'The conditions that killed the bird may have killed the people,' suggested Toby.

'Quite so. I have great hopes that the interior of the cave may tell us something. If these people were cave dwellers they will certainly have left evidence of it. Tomorrow morning we will go and investigate. Once upon a time the conditions here must have been the same as now, or even more congenial. A terrible visitation, a major calamity, may have wrought the havoc. After it had passed the place would return to normal, with all living things, on land and in the water, dead. There are no fish in the water now; but there must have been fish here at one time for you say you found a fossil. If the water became ice, or became very hot, the result would be the same. The fish would die. From the condition of the body Rex found I would say that excessive heat was the cause of the catastrophe. We are told that even now the orbit of this planet takes it uncomfortably close to the Sun. Even a slight variation, therefore, brought about by some change in the galaxy – and we know such things do happen – would put an end to all life, leaving such evidence as Rex has seen.'

'What about the vegetation?' prompted Tiger.

The Professor shrugged. 'That would probably be destroyed at the same time. But seeds deep down in the ground might survive. Brought to the surface by wind erosion they would germinate. Again, seeds could have been carried here. Our friends say they are. The thistles, for example. Whether the disaster here happened ten thousand years ago, or ten million, need not concern us. But we may be sure it happened.

'I should have thought it did concern us,' countered Tiger,

knocking out his pipe, for he was taking full advantage of this opportunity to smoke.

'And what, my dear fellow, do you mean by that?' inquired the Professor.

'I was thinking that the orbit of this particular lump of mud may not be constant. By which I mean that at certain intervals the proximity of another planetoid might change its course so that it passed much nearer to the sun than usual.'

'Well?'

'It struck me that if you persist in this idea of yours, of staying here and taking a ride round the orbit, so to speak, you may strike the very trip when everything is due for its periodical scorching.'

The Professor stared, his spectacles slipping slowly to the end of his nose. 'I didn't think of that,' he confessed. 'But then, the idea came to me before Rex made his startling discoveries. I shall certainly reconsider the project in the light of this unexpected information.'

Vargo, who had been listening intently, now stepped into the conversation. 'The matter did not seem worth mentioning before, but I think I had better tell you now that our new friends, who have been here for several sun-cycles, are of the opinion that at the peak of each successive cycle the heat was greater than on the previous occasion. That can only mean a nearer approach to the Sun. This cycle will be hotter than the last. They believe that eventually, although it may not happen for a long while, this planetoid will, in passing too close to the Sun, be drawn into it, causing one of those scars which are sometimes observed, and which I have heard you call sunspots.'

Silence fell. The Professor combed his untidy hair with his fingers. Tiger refilled his pipe from a pouch that was nearly empty. Toby poked the fire. Rex nibbled a root, rather like a parsnip, which the Andoans had said was good to eat.

'I think,' said the Professor, slowly, at last, 'that the sooner we remove ourselves from this pretty, but apparently unreliable, little world, the better. I would not like to go, though, without seeing with my own eyes, the fascinating relics of the past which Rex has so fortunately found. We will go first thing in the morning. When we return, if Borron is ready, we will proceed on our way home.'

Vargo said he thought it would be the sensible thing to do.

As it was now dark Rex stretched himself out on the warm sand and prepared for sleep. Lying on his back he gazed at a sky ablaze with stars. It was hard to believe that he might have set foot on some of them. It was even harder to believe that he was lying on one at that moment; and that perhaps far away on Earth, an astronomer, with his eye to his telescope, was working out the orbit of the planetoid which they had named Arcadia, but which on Earth was known only by a number.

12 A tragedy of the past

The following morning there was unusual activity in the camp, and daybreak found them, with Vargo in the party, on the way to the cave. Vargo had an idea that the body Rex had found might be that of a castaway Spaceman, but this turned out to be not the case.

Arriving at the ancient river bed Rex showed them the tracks and the fossilized fish, which the Professor declared was a very early form, having fins that were feet to enable it to leave the water and travel overland. Investigation revealed others, notably some large shells embedded in the rock.

They went on to the cave, into which the light of the rising sun was now creeping, giving the place a less repellent atmosphere than when Rex had found it in the afternoon. Torches which they had made were now lighted, and after a pause to allow the Professor to glance at the bones lying about they went inside.

They stopped, of course, at the body, and the Professor went down on his hands and knees to make a thorough examination of it, for naturally he was anxious to determine what manner of man it had been. Even to Rex's amateur eyes this had been no brutish ape-man. With a straight back, broad shoulders and a well-balanced head he might have been a modern athlete. Only the forehead was rather low and the jaw prominent. Looking down at the empty eye sockets Rex found himself wondering on what images they had once gazed, on what strange scenes and uncouth creatures.

The Professor gave it as his opinion that the body had been reduced to its present condition by excessive heat. In fact, he was sure of it, for marks of scorching could still be seen.

Passing on they came to a number of roughly squared pieces of rock that had evidently been used as chairs. It must have been here that hunters had sat to discuss the day's sport, for lying about were implements, mostly of unpolished flint. The odd thought struck Rex that the homes of the earliest Britons must have looked something like this, perhaps at the very time that tragedy came to Arcadia.

As they walked on, slowly, pointing to a weapon here and a dusty earthenware pot there, it soon became clear that the man, the body of whom Rex had found, had not died alone. Others in increasing numbers could be seen lying on the dusty floor. The Professor stopped beside one. 'A woman,' he said, and pointed to a string of shells, a necklace, that she held in her hand. From the way it was held out in front of her it might have been her most cherished possession, which she was determined to save. A little girl wore a bracelet of coloured stones. How little she could have guessed, reflected Rex morbidly, that her little treasure would be gazed upon by men untold ages after she had ceased to be.

'In the female, personal adornment is not a modern habit,' observed the Professor drily.

Still little guessing what lay ahead they came upon an object that brought a cry of amazement to the Professor's lips. It was the body of a man, but in his arms, holding it under him as if for protection, was an animal. Without any doubt whatever it was a dog.

'Well, that *is* a knockout,' muttered Tiger.

'It is something which you, as a hunter, should appreciate,' said the Professor, in a moved voice. 'One day in the dim past, how long ago no one knows and will never know, a man, for the first time, went hunting with an animal by his side – the animal which, by its loyalty and devotion, has drawn nearer to him than any other. A dog. What a partnership that has been! The dog with a nose to scent the game, the speed to bring it to bay and the teeth to hold it until his master ran up with a club to kill it. That was in the days when to eat meant to kill, and failure to kill, death by starvation. Well, in a million years of faith and understanding men and dogs have got to know each other well. Would that all men had the same regard for each other. This poor fellow died trying to save his dog. Let us salute him.'

Moving on, a short distance took them to what turned out to be the end of the cave, and there such a spectacle met their gaze that Rex shrank back in horror. It was packed with bodies. What had happened was plain enough to see. The people, men, women and children, flying from the devastating heat outside, had pressed into the cave until they could go no farther. But there was no escape. The fire demon had followed them in, and there they had died, being, as the Professor averred in an awe-stricken voice, literally roasted to death. And thus had their poor dried-out bodies been preserved.

Rex felt ill with emotion. How many other worlds, civilized or otherwise, had ended like this? he wondered. Would this, one day, be the end of Earth? Trying to dismiss the awful thought, he turned and walked away. The others very soon followed him, and stood to recover their composure just outside the entrance.

'What a terrible, ruthless, merciless thing the Universe is,' said the Professor in a melancholy voice. 'Terrible – terrible – terrible. And what puny creatures we are, to be sure. The lives of these poor wretches were snuffed out like the flame of a candle with no more compassion than the people of Pompeii were snuffed out of existence by the eruption of Vesuvius two thousand years ago. We cry out against hydrogen bombs, and rightly so, for it is not difficult to imagine such a scene as this on Earth should a madman get one in his hands. Yet people go on squabbling and scrambling over trifles with this awful threat hanging over their heads. Amazing, isn't it? Let us go away from this depressing place with its awful picture of inevitable doom. I'm almost sorry you found it, Rex. I would have preferred to take away with me less harrowing memories of what we prematurely named Arcadia.'

In almost funereal procession, oppressed by the drama of what they had seen, they started back for the ship. For a little while Rex was too much a prey to melancholy to pay much attention to personal discomfort but it dawned on him presently that it was exceptionally hot. They sought shade as much as possible, but at times they were forced into the open, and at such times the direct rays of the sun seemed to burn the skin. Even so he gave no serious thought to it, for he knew they were approaching the Sun and that high summer was exceptionally hot. The Andoans had said so. But he had not thought that a single day could make such a difference. More than once he noticed Vargo looking at the sky as though he was puzzled, but he did not question him as to the reason.

It was not until they came in sight of the ship, and he saw everyone in a group staring upward, that he had reason to suppose that something unusual was happening. The others must have realized it, too, for there was a general quickening of the pace. Borron, seeing them coming, beckoned as if the matter was urgent. They needed no other encouragement to hurry.

As they joined the group Borron said something tersely in his own language to Vargo, and he in turn looked up. So did Rex, his eyes on that section of the sky that seemed the focal point of interest. At first he could see nothing clearly on account of the glare of the Sun, but by shading his eyes with his hands he made out an exceptionally bright star close to the Sun. He knew at once that for a star to be seen at all in such conditions, with the naked eye, could only mean that it was of exceptional size. Being so near the Sun it would of course be brilliant.

The Professor said: 'What is it?'

Vargo answered, 'It is the planet which you call Mercury.'

On the face of it there was little in this statement to cause alarm, for Mercury is the planet nearest to the Sun, and so far under the influence of its gravity that it is unable to revolve, and for ever keeps the same side turned towards its mighty parent, as the Moon does to Earth. For the rest, all Rex knew about it was that it had an eccentric orbit, was less than half the size of Earth, and that from Earth it could be seen only at dawn and dusk. Obviously, they were now much closer to it, and therefore closer to the Sun. Which in turn meant that they were a long way from Mino, considerably farther than they had supposed. What had happened was clear. Sitting quietly on Arcadia they had been hurtling towards the Sun at a velocity beyond anything that had been imagined, even by the experts in the party. This accounted for the sudden rise in temperature. In a word, in allowing Arcadia to take them nearer home they had overshot the mark by a considerable margin.

Was Arcadia off its course? Had it, too, an eccentric orbit? Was it on its way to another holocaust? Was its velocity constant, or was it increasing as it neared the gravitational attraction of Mercury, or the Sun? These were the thoughts that flashed through Rex's head as he helped with preparations for departure. From the speed with which these were being made, without even a pause to discuss the situation, it was manifest that the old hands among the professional spacemen did not like the look of things and were anxious to be off. Their alarm was not expressed in words, but Rex could sense it, and it was therefore with relief that he went through the discomfort of acceleration, and presently, through his window, saw the planetoid of mixed memories dropping away below in a sky which, as they shot out of the atmosphere, turned from blue to indigo, and then to black.

Was it on its way to destruction? he mused. He hoped not, for he had spent some happy hours there and had developed a regard for it. Would it survive and return to its normal orbit shorn of its vegetation by the merciless solar rays to start life all over again or would it plunge into the sun and be lost for ever? There was, of course, no answer to these questions, questions really too stupendous for the human mind to grasp.

Tiger must have been thinking on the same lines, for he broke a silence that had lasted for some time by saying: 'I fancy it was a lucky break for you, Professor, that we hadn't already departed, leaving you to take your joyride round Old Fieryface.' He smiled. 'Moral: never take a trip on an unknown orbit.'

'Experience teaches,' answered the Professor tritely. 'After this be sure I never shall. Tell us, Vargo, are we out of danger?'

'I think so.'

'You only *think* so?'

'In space there is always danger,' said Vargo cautiously.

Rex had realized this. On Arcadia he had looked with horror at the damage that had been done to the Andoan ship by the tail of the comet. That was one thing that could happen, and the best pilot in the Universe would be unable to prevent it. Would future travellers risk space travel knowing that that sort of thing could happen? Presumably, it seemed, since the present generation accepted the risks of ordinary air travel, which was not without its hazards from meteorological causes beyond the control of the pilot.

The *Tavona* sped on its way, Rex deriving some comfort from the fact that he was once more in sight of Earth. With its Moon it was conspicuous as a double star. After what he had just seen it was nice to know it was still there, and in his heart he would have welcomed a suggestion to go straight home – just to make sure that nothing awful had happened to it during their absence. But the suggestion was not made. He did not think it would be, for the Professor had left a lot of equipment on Mino and he was unlikely to go home without it. In any case they would have to call at Mars to see how the work there, for which they were to some extent responsible, was going on. At all events, it was something that the risk of being scorched to death appeared to have passed. But had all risks passed? Apparently not, for now that things had settled down Vargo made a statement revealing what may have prompted him to evade a direct answer to the Professor's question about danger.

He began by saying that while there was no immediate cause for alarm, a critical situation might arise as a result of the number of passengers in the ship. The rate of air consumption had, in fact, been almost doubled. Water could be rationed, but not air. The conversion gear would not be able to translate back into oxygen such an excessive amount of carbon dioxide as would inevitably be produced. The supply of air was getting low when they had landed on Arcadia. While on the planetoid there had been ample for them to breathe, but it could not be stored; and to complicate matters they were farther from Mino than they had ever expected to be, the result of underestimating their velocity. The present situation had been foreseen, but it had not been mentioned, Vargo said, because had the Andoans learned of it they would, as a matter of honour, have refused to jeopardize the lives of the whole party even though by remaining on Arcadia they would be certain to perish. But one of the first laws of space travel, Vargo asserted, was all or none.

'Quite right,' broke in the Professor.

Wherefore, continued Vargo, their extra passengers had

not yet been informed of the true state of affairs or they might still demand to be put back on Arcadia. They would regard that as the honourable thing to do. But the Minoans had a sense of honour, too, and for that reason had kept silent on the principle of all or none. However, the future was by no means hopeless. There was ample compressed air to see a limited number of the crew home, so should things become serious, if a planetoid could be found with a reasonable atmosphere, some of the passengers would be put off, to be picked up later after the ship had returned to Mino to re-charge its tanks and cylinders. As a matter of fact, Vargo concluded, Borron had considered taking the ship home while they were on Arcadia, leaving everyone there, until he became suspicious of the increasing temperature taken in conjunction with unusual movements among the stars, although this, it was now realized, was due to the phenomenal velocity of Arcadia itself. Borron would now put the position to the Andoans.

It was plain when he did so that the visitors had something to say about it, although Rex little suspected what it was. It transpired that they had good news. Over a long period of time their Exploration Fleet had been making dumps of air cylinders and provisions at various points for just such an emergency as the present one. All ships' officers knew where these dumps were, although as a matter of fact they had never – as far as the Andoans knew – been needed. Their navigator would take the ship to the nearest.

This welcome information put an entirely different complexion on the situation. Rex remembered the old saying: 'There's nothing new under the sun' when he recalled that in the old sailing ship days on Earth, Admiralty Survey Ships made similar dumps on remote islands for the benefit of mariners cast away on them. Actually, they went even further, putting ashore such livestock as goats, pigs and even rabbits.

With these thoughts passing through his mind he watched with fascinated admiration Borron and the Andoan Navigation Officer plotting their course by the stars. They seemed to know every constellation and every unit of it. It was, of course, their job, and they had been doing it for years, yet even so it amazed him when he looked at the thousand points of light that spangled the sky that they should know every one and have a name for it. A sailor, he mused, might recognize a particular piece of coast, or a lighthouse; but he was never called upon to look at a vast tangle of them at one time. Space pilots on Earth, presumably, when that time came, would be faced with the formidable task of learning their 'stars'.

It was with pardonable impatience that he awaited their arrival at the new objective, whereon was the dump on which so much depended. Vargo assured them that there would be no difficulty in finding the stores for their position was always marked with a high white pole set in a circle of white-painted boulders, the whole thing in the largest available open space. He said, too, that the planetoids selected for these stores were chosen for their positions on the regular space routes rather than for living amenities. For it was not intended that crews should stay at these places, but simply pick up what stores were required as occasion demanded.

It turned out that there was no question of their remaining on this particular store-planet. They did not even land.

Even from a distance it was apparent from the frown that furrowed Borron's forehead that something was wrong; that something was different from what he expected. The shining white light of the planetoid's reflection, he said, could only mean that it was enveloped in dense white cloud. What had caused this was unimportant. It meant that they would be unable to land.

The cloud turned out to be a thick belt of carbon dioxide.

Where it had come from was a matter for surmise. It must have been of comparatively recent formation, for stores would not have been laid down in such conditions. It was a bitter disappointment, for as Vargo said, there was no doubt about the much-needed stores being there. The fact that the cloud was composed of poison gas was not the trouble. They would have been safe in their spacesuits. The real difficulty was, with visibility nil they had no hope of finding the dump. It might be anywhere. They had reckoned on spotting it from above and landing beside it. A haphazard landing, trusting to luck, was out of the question. The dump might be miles from the spot where they touched down, and space-suits, while efficient for short journeys, were never intended for long distance work.

'So what do we do?' asked Tiger.

'We must go on and hope for better luck next time,' answered Vargo.

The Professor took a small paper bag from his pocket. 'Would anyone like a caramel?' he asked calmly.

13 All or none

Conditions in the *Tavona* were still fairly comfortable when, remaining on a general course for Mino, they reached the next objective. They were making ultimately for Mino because it was there that the Professor had left much of his equipment, including undeveloped photographic film which he was naturally anxious to collect.

From above, the planetoid, when they came within sight of it, looked a black, cold place, mostly rock, with grey plains covered with what appeared to be moss or lichen. A test showed that there was practically no atmosphere – just faint traces of helium. It was a small place, having a diameter of only a few miles.

Three times Borron circumnavigated the inhospitable globe on a zig-zag course while all eyes watched from the windows seeking the white pole.

They failed to find it.

'Are you sure this is the right place?' asked the Professor.

'Quite sure,' answered Vargo.

Borron took the ship down to a few feet and continued the search, quartering the ground to make sure that every square yard of it was covered.

It was Tiger who first spotted a white object and called attention to it. Borron took the ship directly over it. It was the pole – or a piece of it. Smaller pieces lay about, splintered, on the front edge of what looked like a glacial moraine. Behind, at a steep incline, rose a great mass of boulders and detritus. What had happened was all too plain to see.

Vargo, in his usual dispassionate voice, said: 'There has been a landslide. The dump has been buried.'

For some seconds no other comment was made. It was quite obvious, and therefore unnecessary to say, that to start to move the mass, rock by rock, hoping to find the dump, was futile. Even if by an amazing stroke of luck they did find it, it would certainly have been crushed flat.

'Now what?' asked Rex, in a hollow voice.

'We must go on,' replied Vargo. 'There is nothing else we can do.'

The ship swung away to resume a quest that was beginning to look hopeless. Borron's expression did not change but Rex noticed that he was now looking more and more often at his gauges. No need to ask why.

Before long the atmosphere in the ship was becoming noticeably unpleasant. Everyone must have been aware of it, certainly the Andoans, who now asked to be put overboard. They were the intruders, they said. Without them the others would have a better chance.

Borron refused. 'All or none,' he said curtly. 'I am the captain of this ship.'

Rex suggested that those who had spacesuits should put them on, and by using their individual air supply conserve what was in the ship.

Borron rejected the proposal.

Vargo explained. The cylinders attached to the spacesuits constituted their special reserve. When the time came they would be opened at intervals so that all could share.

Rex said no more.

The atmosphere was, he knew, fast deteriorating. He also knew that nothing could be done about it. He had known from the outset that the failure of oxygen apparatus was one of the main risks of space travel, and it now looked as if this was to be their fate. One day, perhaps in a million years, millions of miles away, someone would find the ship and wonder who they were.

They were all beginning to suffer from the first pangs of suffocation when the next store base was reached. There, plain to see, was the pole that meant salvation. But alas, when they staggered out, gasping, into a thin, strange-smelling atmosphere, all that remained of the cylinders was a heap of rust. Something, apparently, had acted on the metal and eaten through it. For Rex, this third disappointment was the last straw. This, he thought, must be the end. There was an atmosphere on the planetoid but not enough to support life for long.

Borron ordered everyone back into the ship.

Vargo said they had one chance left. At no great distance away, the Andoan navigator had told him, there was a planetoid with a reasonable atmosphere. If they could reach it, Borron and one other man would go on alone, leaving them there, to return as quickly as possible. If they failed to reach it . . . Vargo shrugged his shoulders.

'Don't forget we have oxygen in the spacesuit cylinders,' reminded Rex.

'If we use that *no one* will get home,' said Vargo simply. 'Borron will need it to get to Mino.'

Now began a nightmare journey. No one spoke. No one moved. They sat still, staring at each other, taking long, quick breaths as their lungs fought for the oxygen that was not there. The scene began to blur in front of Rex's eyes. His jaw sagged. So this was what suffocation was like.

On Borron's order one of the crew opened a spacesuit valve. This brought relief, but Rex felt it was only postponing the inevitable end. The awful feeling of suffocation returned. He began to gasp. The inside of the ship was growing dark and he slumped forward, his head between his hands. In a vague sort of way he saw Toby slide quietly to the floor.

When the ship's legs bumped he was hardly aware of it, but when cold sweet air suddenly poured into his lungs and he looked up to see that the doors were open, he could hardly believe his eyes; and it took his reeling faculties some seconds to grasp the fact that they had landed. Some of the crew were applying artificial respiration to the others. Vargo was working on Toby who appeared to be dead, although, as it transpired, he was only unconscious. Tiger lurched to the door and fell out. Rex followed him, to stagger, stumble and fall flat, sucking in air in great gulps. All he could think was, they had reached the objective, they were saved – for the time being, at any rate. That was enough to go on with. He was satisfied to be out of the ship, which had become a death chamber.

In a few minutes, such was the swift effect of the life-giving air, they were all practically back to normal, although somewhat pale from shock and reaction.

'Dear – dear. That was a near thing,' observed the Professor, peering at the others over his spectacles.

'If we ever have a nearer it'll be the last,' asserted Toby grimly.

There was no dump on Vana, as Borron called their haven of refuge, the reason being, the Andoans had told him, because an atmosphere made one unnecessary. Anyone land-ing there could survive without artificial aid until a rescue party arrived, although it might be a long time before that happened.

This meant that Borron would have to rely on the oxygen in the cylinders of the spacesuits in order to reach home. With only two persons on board, himself and the navigator, starting with a ship full of sweet air that would last them for some time, he hoped to get through, although this was by no means certain. He would start forthwith and get back as quickly as possible. There was no point in delaying departure.

Rex watched the preparations being made, aware that Borron and his companion had accepted an awful risk without hesitation. If the air supply proved insufficient their fate was a foregone conclusion. Some of their few remaining stores, foodstuffs, water and emergency capsules, were put out. Tiger collected his rifle, saying he felt uncomfortable without it. If he left it in the ship it might fall into hands which, not understanding the purpose of it, could do some damage.

As Borron, without any dramatic farewells, entered the ship, Rex went over to him. 'If you get home all right you might give Morino my kind regards,' he said, with deliberate nonchalance to cover his embarrassment.

Borron said he would. 'She will be angry with me for coming home without you,' he said, with a suspicion of a smile.

Those who were to remain, standing on a little sandy plain dotted with tufts of coarse grass, watched the ship go, watched it until, swiftly diminishing in size, it was lost to sight in the great ocean of space over their heads. As it went up so Rex's stomach seemed to go down, for he could not cast off the fear that he might never see it again. If Borron reached home all would no doubt be well; but should he fail there would be no other prospect than all of them ending their days on the sphere on which they stood, lost for eternity in the infinite void. Why it should seem more terrible to die on a planetoid in space than on a remote island in an Earthly ocean he did not know; but there it was.

With such depressing thoughts as these laying a cold hand on his heart he gazed around to see on what sort of world they had been marooned. Good or bad there had been no choice; and whatever else it might lack it had at least an atmosphere, a thin one judging from the temperature, which was too cold to be comfortable, although, as he perceived, this might be due to the time, which was dawn. He hoped, and thought, it would become warmer as the sun rose – or to be accurate, when the planetoid turned its full face to the Sun.

A preliminary inspection was far from reassuring. A more dreary, desolate landscape he had never seen – at all events, on a world boasting an atmosphere. Under a sky of pale mauve, as far as he could see in one direction rolled an undulating wilderness of black volcanic sand, littered with clinkers, pieces of shell, and with outcrops of grey pumice-stone, as full of holes as a honeycomb. The only living vegetation, apart from some tufts of coarse, spiky, dead-looking grass, was a bloated growth of cactus, purple in colour with dark green berries.

In the opposite direction was a field of pumice, piled in ridges, like waves, as it had solidified from its original form of liquid lava. Beyond this rose a savage-looking massif, cloven by ravines, as black as coal except where it was stained with livid streaks of red and yellow. Around the top of this formidable mass of rock floated wreaths of vapour, smoke or cloud, it was not known which. That the whole place had once been subjected to great heat was apparent. Over it all, weighing on the ground like a blanket, hung a heavy, brooding silence. If ever a place told visitors that they were not wanted, this one certainly did, mused Rex.

A movement caught his eyes, causing him to start, for so far he had seen no living thing, and in view of the nature of the planetoid, did not expect to see one.

It was a crab, a fairly large one, emerging slowly from the sand. Its shell was bright yellow, and its protruding goggle eyes, and mouth set vertically instead of horizontally, gave it a most diabolical expression of ferocity. Drawing clear of the sand it stood up on its hind legs and waved its claws threateningly.

'I see we have company,' remarked the Professor, cynically.

'A most unattractive little monster, too. I wonder why he hid in the sand.'

'To keep warm during the night, which must have been chilly, as it's chilly now,' suggested Tiger.

'I'd say it's more likely that he was afraid of something,' returned the Professor. 'As you must have observed on our travels, where there is one form of life there is usually another. In some cases, I suspect, there may have been several, but that law of nature which insists on the survival only of the fittest reduces the number to two or three.'

'A good many have survived on Earth,' Rex pointed out.

'Yes, but look at the size of Earth, and its great variety of physical conditions, compared with the average planetoid. Everything must eat, and on a place this size, the weaker, those unable to fight, have small chance of escape. It would be safe to say, I think, that the smaller the world the fewer the varieties of life likely to be found on it.'

'Let us hope the crabs are good to eat. They'll help out the stores,' put in Toby, practically.

'If there is life there should be water somewhere, so as soon as we have settled on a spot to make camp we should start looking for it,' advised Vargo.

To this proposal they all agreed.

For their camp they could find no better place than where they were. The terrain was the same everywhere as far as they could see on their side of the planetoid. There was no cover, not even a tree. Thinking of a gully or a cave they looked at the massif, but even as they considered walking to it a great shoulder of rock broke away and went crashing down in a ground-shaking landslide. A cloud of dust went up. Some of the boulders, bounced far across the pale-coloured pumice-stone. It was clear that in the proximity of the big rock mass was no place to settle down.

At Vargo's suggestion the party broke into three groups

to explore the ground more quickly. The Andoans went to the left. The original ship's crew, with the exception of Vargo, went to the right. Vargo led the rest straight forward. The sun was now well above the horizon, and while it was smaller than when seen from Earth – they were of course farther away from it – its rays, unopposed by a wide belt of atmosphere, were both bright and warm. Later in the day they became fierce enough to cause the Professor to warn the others to beware of sunstroke.

Rex's party found no water. They could see where there had been some in the deep hollows, suggesting a slight rainfall, but the soft rock, as porous as blotting paper, had absorbed it. Being soft it was dangerous stuff to walk on, often breaking away under the slightest pressure to the risk of broken limbs. Eventually, with the sun falling again towards the horizon, the party turned back without finding water, food, or anything else of interest. They could see the other two parties also returning.

They got back to their base to find the ground crawling with crabs.

Rex looked at them with disgust. 'Sleeping here isn't going to be funny if those little horrors start crawling over us,' he muttered. 'If they come out at sunset they may stay around all night.'

'The question is, what do they live on?' said Toby.

No one attempted to guess the answer, for at this juncture the other two parties arrived, the Andoans to report, through Vargo, that they had found nothing, and the Minoans to make the astonishing assertion that there were little men on the planet.

Everyone stared. 'Little men?' echoed the Professor.

'They say so,' said Vargo.

'What exactly do they mean by little men?' demanded the Professor.

Vargo put the question, and receiving a reply held a hand about two feet above the ground to indicate the height of the men.

Tiger laughed – a trifle uneasily. 'It isn't true,' he declared.

Vargo said these men had no hair on their bodies. They walked upright, and leapt from rock to rock with great agility.

'It looks as if you've got another new species for your list, Professor,' said Toby.

'I'll believe in these midget men when I see one,' stated Rex recklessly.

Toby pointed. 'Take a look,' said he, in a curious voice.

They all turned in the direction indicated.

Standing bolt upright on a slab of rock about twenty yards away was one of the 'little men'.

'That isn't a man, it's a monkey!' cried Rex. But his voice lacked conviction. 'At least,' he added dubiously, 'I hope it's a monkey.'

The truth was, the creature looked as much like a miniature man as a monkey, possibly because it had no hair – and no tail.

14 Out of
the frying-pan...

Instead of fur, as would be expected of a normal monkey, the creature had a light brown leathery-looking skin. Its eyes, regarding them with an interest as great as their own, were dark, and steady with a disconcerting intelligence. In its hand it held either a long slither of rock or a petrified stick. All these factors gave it a horribly human appearance. The only thing against it being human was its size. Had it been as tall as a man Rex would have had no hesitation in believing it to be one – of sorts. Perhaps a very primitive form of savage.

Beyond it, a veritable army of the creatures could be seen approaching from the direction of the massif.

'Well, we've seen some monstrosities, but that one is the tops,' asserted Toby.

The animal looked directly at him and chattered something that sounded like a string of words.

'Heavens above!' exclaimed the Professor. 'I believe it's talking.'

'The crabs don't like his language, anyway,' remarked Tiger. 'Look at them!'

Every crab was digging itself into the sand with unbelievable speed.

'I don't know that I quite like this,' said Tiger seriously, picking up his rifle. 'These little horrors may be small, but if the whole mob came for us things would look ugly.'

No one answered. What Tiger had said was all too true.

Fear of such a situation passed as the leader of the band now revealed why he had come to the sand – and why the crabs were removing themselves from the surface of it with the greatest possible speed.

Running forward with nimble agility the monkey snatched up a crab by the claw, dexterously avoiding the gaping pincers, and hurled it against a rock with such force that the shell split wide open. Taking it up again the monkey tore it into two halves. This exposed the meat in the shell, as was the intention, for it was promptly scooped out and eaten. Then, to the astonishment of the beholders, the monkey cracked the claws between two pieces of rock and ate the contents of those, too.

The noise of this operation must have told its companions what was going on, for they now rushed forward, and in an orgy of splintering shells, snarling and spitting, there began a feast that was not pretty to watch.

'So that's the idea,' said Tiger. 'Well, at least we know what *they* eat,' he added whimsically.

In a few minutes the party was surrounded with hundreds of monkeys all busily engaged with what, from the old shells littered about, was a regular meal.

There was one touch of comedy to enliven the rather disgusting proceedings. Rex had admired the adroit way the monkeys avoided the menacing claws as they picked up the crabs, due, no doubt to long practice. But it seemed they were not beyond making a mistake, for with a shriek of anguish one sprang high into the air with a crab hanging on its hand. And apparently the crab had no intention of letting go.

It was the fury of the monkey that was so funny. Howling and cursing it leapt about trying to shake the thing off – and a monkey is never so funny as when it loses its temper. This one did. It succeeded finally in releasing itself from what must have been a painful handshake by the simple expedient of bashing the crab on an outcrop of rock with enough force to kill it. For some time the wretched monkey sat nursing its injured hand, alternately sobbing and mouthing with rage. The others paid not the slightest attention, from which it could be presumed that such misadventures were not uncommon.

There was this about it. To everyone's relief they paid no attention to the invaders of their domain – at any rate, not until the banquet was over when the leader came near and surveyed them with undisguised curiosity. It also had a good look at the heap of stores, as if suspecting the nature of the contents. But it made no attempt to interfere, and after a while retired to a high rock from which to watch over the proceedings.

'I don't think they'll worry us,' decided Tiger.

'Our policy is to leave them severely alone,' said the Professor. 'On no account must we do anything to antagonize them, for their numbers alone could create a nasty situation.'

As things turned out this was easier said than done.

Darkness came swiftly, and everyone disposed himself as he thought best to pass the short night. Rex did not get much sleep. Not only was it intensely cold but the monkeys remained in the vicinity, so that all night long the cracking and crunching of shells went on. To him the miracle was, with this sort of thing going on day after day, how any crabs survived. It struck him, revolting though the idea was at first, that, if the monkeys could eat the crabs without ill effects, they might eat them, too, to eke out the rations. The monkeys retired, just before dawn, to the massif where it seemed they spent most of the day.

The next day was a repetition of the first, except that the monkeys – Rex preferred to think of them as monkeys although their hairless skins made them look even more human than the common run of monkeys – showed a greater interest in them.

If, originally, they had had any fears, they no longer had them, for they advanced uncomfortably close when they saw the visitors eating. It seemed that they had enough intelligence to know that the food came from the heap of stores, for such an interest did they take in them that Tiger had to shoo the precocious little beasts away. They did not go far. Sitting in a closely packed circle, they held, judging from the noise, something in the nature of a conference, the leader addressing the crowd with the fiery eloquence of a soap-box orator in Hyde Park.

The next day they were even more daring, and it was with some difficulty that they were driven off. By now it was clear to everyone that unless the ship returned soon there was going to be trouble.

'I'm afraid we shall have to give these interfering little rascals a lesson,' opined Tiger, irritably, for he had narrowly escaped being bitten in the calf of the leg by a monkey that had refused to budge when ordered to leave the stores.

His fears were confirmed the very next day when a monkey, more audacious than the rest, made a grab at the Professor's camera, which had been left lying on the ground after he had used it. It would have got away with it, too, had not Rex snatched up a stone, and throwing it scored a hit. The monkey dropped his loot, but that was far from being the end of the affair. Not only did the little wretch pick up the stone and throw it back but several of his near companions found missiles and employed the same method of retaliation, so that for a little while pieces of rock, fortunately mostly small, fairly rained about the camp. Tiger was all for showing the throwers that he could handle larger pieces with greater accuracy, but the Professor ordered him to desist.

'We must avoid war if we can,' he declared. 'All reprisals do is invite fresh reprisals. As a military man, Group-Captain, you should know that.'

'I also know that attack is the best method of defence,' answered Tiger curtly.

'Tut-tut. Let us not argue about it,' requested the Professor. 'Let us try pacifist methods first.'

The incident was sufficient to show that if the monkeys really attacked in force, with determination, things would be very awkward indeed, to say the least; and Rex, for one, began to hope that the return of the ship would not be long delayed. Aside from the monkeys, although the Andoans and Minoans consumed very little, the supplies of food and water were getting perilously low.

The next day the monkeys arrived earlier than usual, and from the noise they made as they approached it was clear that they were in a nasty mood and bent on mischief. They paid no attention to the crabs but advanced purposefully in a body towards the invaders. It was reckoned there were not fewer than two hundred of them. Tiger said if they came too close he would fire a shot from his rifle to see if the report had any effect. He had only a handful of cartridges, so if the worst came to the worst there would be no question of destroying the entire army.

Vargo and the Professor agreed that this was all they could do.

Standing upright the monkeys continued to advance, and as they drew near extended their order, the flanks swinging round into a crescent formation. There was no longer any doubt as to what was intended.

'I wouldn't let them get too close or it may be too late to do anything,' said Toby.

Tiger waited until the front rank was not more than thirty yards away; then, raising the rifle to his shoulder, he took quick aim at a rock and fired.

The shot had the desired effect – or so at first it seemed. The report and the shrill whine of the ricocheting bullet as it struck the rock sent the whole pack tearing away in a blind panic. But they did not go far, having the intelligence, perhaps, to realize that the noise had done them no injury. At a distance of a hundred yards they formed in a circle round their leader to discuss the matter – or so it seemed from the chattering. The conference lasted for about half an hour, when, as if a decision had been reached, the horde began again to approach.

'It looks as if I shall have to give the little fools a sterner lesson,' opined Tiger reluctantly.

'These are no ordinary monkeys,' declared Toby. 'They really work things out. If the pugnacious little devils make a serious charge we've had it.'

The truth of this was all too apparent, for as Rex perceived, the weakness of the defenders lay in the fact that they had only one weapon between them – the rifle. Even with cudgels it might have been possible to drive off the attacking force, causing such casualties as to make the monkeys think again about what they were doing. With nothing in his hands Rex had never felt so helpless. It is true there were some pieces of rock lying about but it was mostly small stuff, light and flimsy at that.

Again Tiger raised his rifle. Again it cracked. A monkey in the front rank leapt high into the air, and fell, howling. Dead silence fell on the monkey army; and the sudden hush, after the noise, seemed to carry an even more sinister threat. The only sound was the moaning of the wounded beast.

'That has stopped 'em for a bit,' said Tiger. 'I wish they'd go away. This is a bit too much like murder for my liking.'

Some monkeys picked up their wounded comrade and carried him to the rear. The rest remained where they were, clearly in a state of indecision.

'I'm afraid they'll come on again when they've recovered from the shock you've given them,' said the Professor. 'If our position was not so vulnerable the whole thing would be quite ridiculous.'

Another half-hour passed without any change. Tiger did not shoot again. The sun was now nearing the horizon.

'I hope they're not waiting till it's dark,' said Rex, in a worried voice. 'They seem to be able to see in the dark. How about moving everything nearer to that dry grass. By setting fire to it we should be able to see what we are doing – and what game the monkeys get up to.'

It was agreed that this was a good idea and the stores were accordingly moved nearer to the grass – an operation that was watched by the monkeys with profound interest. By the time the job was done darkness was closing in. An uncomfortable silence fell. There was of course no moonlight as moonlight is understood on Earth, but a faint light was cast by some distant stars, and planetoids that were still catching the Sun. Gentle rustling sounds from the direction of the enemy position revealed that the monkeys were moving.

'If they come with a rush they'll be on us before we see them,' said Tiger.

'I was thinking the same thing,' returned the Professor. 'You'd better put a light to the grass.'

Tiger complied, and the effect surpassed all expectations, for more reasons than one. In the first place the grass blazed up as if it had at one time been soaked in kerosene, so that all hands had to put in some quick work to save the stores. The second effect, just as surprising, was the behaviour of the monkeys. They acted as if the mere sight of fire had sent them crazy. They certainly knew what fire was, possibly as a result of living on volcanic ground, for without waiting for the flames to get near them they fled, screaming and shrieking in paroxysms of terror.

Nobody spoke until the din of the rout had died away in the distance. Then Tiger, turning to the others with an expression of astonishment on his face, remarked: 'Well, that certainly did the trick. What the dickens came over them?'

'They may have more reason to be afraid than we suspect,' averred the Professor thoughtfully.

Nobody paid much attention to this observation at the time. They all stood by the stores watching the flames spreading literally like wildfire. A lurid glow lit up the sky. Clouds of black smoke billowed upwards. The landscape became an inferno.

'I've heard of setting the world on fire and I seem to have done that,' joked Tiger.

'That, I think, is what you have done,' returned the Professor uneasily. 'If you have, my dear fellow, it will be nothing to joke about.'

It took Rex a moment to fully grasp the peril. 'You mean, if the smoke comes down it will choke us?'

'And if it goes up to form a blanket round the whole globe how will Borron find us? He may not even look for us, supposing us to have perished in the conflagration.'

'That's a nasty thought,' said Toby. 'Lucky we made camp on the sand, and not amongst the grass,' he added, as tongues of flame began licking up the face of the massif. 'No wonder the monkeys were scared. Great Scott! Look at that,' he concluded, as the summit of the massif became wrapped for a moment in a sheet of blue flame.

'Those clouds we saw must have been hydrogen,' stated the Professor. 'It looks as if we've jumped out of the monkey-pan into the fire.'

No one thought of sleep. They all stood watching the fire, wondering how far it would spread. What lay on the far side of the planetoid they did not know. If it happened to be rock or sand, the flames, they supposed, would be checked. Someone made a remark to that effect.

The Professor scooped up a handful of sand and squeezed

it through his fingers. 'I'm by no means sure of that,' he startled Rex by saying. 'If this sand doesn't contain oil I've never felt oil-bearing deposits. Given enough heat it will burn. That field of old lava, which Rex called pumice-stone, has so far saved us.'

Nothing more was said. There appeared to be nothing more to say. It was obvious that they had started a fire which nothing could put out. Whether it would die of its own accord, or burn the surface off the globe, only time would show. And after one reek of smoke had come their way it was equally obvious that only the early return of the ship could save them.

Dawn revealed a black smouldering plain between them and the massif, the flames having passed on beyond it. What had become of the monkeys was a matter for surmise. That they would continue to flee before the conflagration was certain, so their survival would appear to depend on their finding an area where the fire had nothing to consume. The Professor thought that if such a place existed they would know of it.

Meanwhile they watched, with what apprehension can be imagined, the smoke-haze thickening above them. They also surveyed the horizon opposite from the one toward which the fire had sped, in case, having circumnavigated the globe, it should come back on them from that direction.

And that in fact was what was about to happen, as a pillar of smoke rising above the skyline foretold.

'I'm afraid this is it,' remarked Toby calmly, as the smoke began to drift towards them.

What made Rex look up he did not know, for his attention, like that of the others, had been concentrated on the horizon. A triumphant yell broke from his lips as he saw the *Tavona* just over their heads, dropping towards them. Even the taciturn Andoans smiled.

'You were only just in time,' Vargo told Borron, as the doors opened and he stepped down.

Borron replied to the effect that he had seen from afar off that something was wrong and hardly expected to find them alive. What had happened?

'You can tell him about it on the way home,' the Professor advised Vargo. 'Let us waste no more time here.'

In a few minutes the *Tavona* was beyond the reach of danger. Rex observed that quite a large area which looked like rock had escaped the disaster, and it was there, he hoped, that the monkeys had found refuge.

15 The man eater of Mars

The journey back to Mino was made without trouble of any sort, and with the planetoid swiftly growing larger as they dropped towards it the voyagers had reason to suppose that their adventures were at an end; for while they were not exactly 'home' there would be no more landings on strange new worlds – not on this occasion, anyway. Only Mars now lay on their route to Earth. Moreover, the Professor had stated his intention of returning to Glensalich Castle forthwith, as he was anxious to develop his photographs and write up his notes while events were still fresh in his mind. The only reason they had looked in on Mino, apart from putting off the Andoans, was to collect certain equipment and personal baggage which had been left there.

A little crowd had collected to see the *Tavona* land, for until Borron's belated return for stores, the ship, long overdue, had been given up for lost, to the grief of Morino, who was among those present to greet the explorers.

Two days it was thought would be ample time to complete their business on Mino. They would then, it was arranged, proceed home in the *Tavona*, calling at Mars on the way to see how the work of restoration was going on. After the things that had happened to them this all sounded very simple, but like so many simple projects it did not work out according to plan.

The first piece of information Morino gave Rex was that Rolto was also on the missing list. He had departed without orders for an unknown destination and had not been heard of since. The High Council were very angry about it. Rex, somewhat rashly as it transpired, said he couldn't care less.

The second item of news seemed much more important. The work of reconstruction on Mars had been held up by the appearance of a monstrous white beast the like of which no man had ever seen before. Its savage nature was exceeded only by its appetite. Making its home in the forest near Utopia, having killed the imported poultry, it emerged every day to carry off one of the workers, torturing its victim before killing and eating him. Things had come to such a pass that no one dare go out. The beast was as active by night as by day. At night everyone bolted himself in one of the houses while the monster prowled the streets making the most blood-curdling noises. In short, Mars was going through a Reign of Terror.

'Sounds like the Maneater of Tsavo all over again,' remarked the Professor. 'You may remember how the construction of the Cape to Cairo railway was actually brought to a standstill by man-eating lions which carried off victims night after night until Colonel Patterson tackled the brutes single-handed and disposed of them one by one. He afterwards wrote a book about it – the classic of all big game hunting stories. It rather looks, my dear Group-Captain, as if you have been provided with an opportunity of indulging in your favourite sport by following in the footsteps of the gallant Colonel.'

'I'll certainly see what I can do about it,' promised Tiger. 'I'd say the whole thing has been exaggerated.'

How wrong he was in this opinion was in due course to be demonstrated.

The third and final incident on Mino was more distressing than alarming. When they came to pack their kit certain items were found to be missing, notably Tiger's spare suit of clothes and some shoes. Some books could not be found.

This discovery was all the more painful because it had always been understood that on Mino theft was unknown. When Vargo was told of it he at first refused to believe it, and when proof was provided his astonishment and disappointment was as great as theirs. Nothing could be done about it. There were no police to make enquiries. Tiger glossed over the affair, saying that as they were going home the matter was unimportant, so rather than make a fuss that would embarrass everyone, including the High Council, he was prepared to forget about it. The puzzling thing was why anyone should want his clothes, for it would be impossible for the thief to wear them without betraying himself. In the light of subsequent events it may seem strange that no one guessed the solution to the mystery; but the fact remains, no one did.

Anyway, in due course farewells were said, with more tears from Morino, although Rex assured her that he would soon be coming back. The Andoans tried to persuade them to go home with them and see the wonders of their world, assuring them of a warm welcome. The Professor declined the invitation with reluctance, saying that at the moment he hadn't time for such a long trip; but he accepted it for some future date. So, with friendly wishes for a safe journey and a quick return still ringing in their ears the visitors took their places in the ship that had carried them so far and were soon watching the big planetoid drop away below.

When they arrived on Mars it was at once evident that even if the size of the Terror had been exaggerated its effect on the morale of the workmen had not, for there wasn't a soul in sight, either at the canal or in the town. Some men came out when the ship landed, however, and in a long conversation gave Vargo a detailed description of the menace and its behaviour. This he passed on to the others.

The beast, he said, had four legs, was nearly as tall as a

man and covered with white fur. It had terrible teeth and claws, and its strength was such that it could not only carry a man in its mouth but gallop away with him. It lived in the forest and was never far away. It was afraid of nothing. But then, as Tiger pointed out, as the workmen were unarmed the beast had nothing to be afraid of. A heavy soft-nosed bullet should give it other ideas.

'It still sounds a pretty tall story to me,' he concluded sceptically, as he picked up his rifle and put some cartridges in his pocket.

'Just a minute,' put in Rex, taking Vargo by the arm and pointing. 'Forgive me for changing the subject but isn't that Rolto's blue-starred ship over there? In the next square.'

'Yes,' replied Vargo, looking puzzled. 'That is his ship. What can he be doing here?'

'He was reported missing. It looks as if he might have been here all the time.'

'What I would like to know is why he came here,' said Vargo, looking around. 'Where is he? He must have seen us land. Why is he keeping out of sight? Has he another mad scheme in his head? But I see some of his crew over there. I will go and have a word with them while Tiger is hunting this alleged monster.'

Tiger's method of dealing with the beast was the normal one. With the loaded rifle in the crook of his arm he started walking cautiously towards the forest, his eyes alert for the first sign of movement. Actually, as he said afterwards, he did not expect the animal to show itself.

The Professor did not share his confidence. 'Be careful,' he warned. 'Don't let us have an accident, just as we are going home.'

'I'm not going into the timber, if that's what you mean,' returned Tiger. 'That would be asking for trouble. At the moment I'm merely hoping that the creature will give us a glimpse of itself, so that I shall know what I have to deal with.'

The others followed for a little distance but then Tiger asked them to stop. They might get in the way. It would be better if they remained within reach of the buildings just in case the creature turned nasty. So they waited in a group, watching, while he walked on alone.

For a little while it looked as if they were going to be disappointed. Then Rex spotted a white object moving slowly in the undergrowth, just inside the forest, and knew it could only be the Terror. But, as he remarked, as Tiger also saw it and turned towards it, it was nothing like as tall as a man. The description had been exaggerated, as descriptions so often are. As far as it was possible to judge the thing was no taller than a dog.

But when suddenly the beast rose up and bounded into the open he gasped, realizing that it must have been crouching in a stalking attitude. It was a colossal cat.

What the animal actually was must have been apparent to all of them, but it was Rex who cried in a strangled voice: 'It's the kitten – the kitten I was taking to Morino – grown enormous. I lost it here and left it behind. It must have caught the same disease as—'

His voice trailed away to silence as the monster settled itself down in the familiar manner of a house cat about to spring on a bird or a mouse. But there the resemblance to a tame cat ended. Its eyes blazed and its lips parted showing fangs that a lion might have envied. To say that Rex was shaken would hardly describe his sensations. Little wonder, he thought, that the wretched unarmed workmen had been scared stiff, and unable to cope with the horror.

Everyone held his breath as Tiger brought the rifle to his shoulder and took aim. It seemed seconds before the weapon crashed. With a terrifying snarl the beast rose up on its hind legs, biting at its shoulder where the bullet must have struck. It fell, and for a moment Rex thought it was all over. But no. Getting on its feet again the great cat charged.

Tiger stood his ground. Not that he had any alternative, for running would not save him. Again he fired, but if the bullet went home the animal gave no sign of it. He jerked another cartridge into the breech and fired again. Still the beast came on.

Rex went cold all over. Was the brute invulnerable? He knew the shots must be hitting the creature. Why didn't they stop it?

From ten yards the cat made its final spring. Tiger fired at it in the air, leapt aside, and as it landed on the spot where he had stood put the muzzle of the rifle almost into its ear and pulled the trigger. Rex, who had subconsciously been counting, knew it was the last cartridge in his magazine.

Tiger backed away, reloading swiftly. But he need not have troubled. The animal that was to have been a pet was on its side. For a few seconds it tore at the ground with its claws, then lay still. Tiger gave it one more shot to make quite sure; then, with the rifle again in the crook of his arm he walked back to where the others were waiting.

'Sorry I had to kill your kitten, Rex, but it was the only thing to do,' he said cheerfully.

Rex went limp as his strung-up nerves relaxed. 'My goodness!' he breathed. 'You gave me a fright.'

Tiger smiled. 'I gave myself one if it comes to that. I wasn't expecting anything that size.'

'It must have been eating some carrion that had died from your special insecticide, Professor,' opined Toby.

'The moral seems to be, let us bring no more carnivorous animals to Mars,' said the Professor seriously, looking at them over his spectacles.

Tiger was filling his pipe. 'If a kitten could do that, I'd

hate to meet a lion that had been here for a week or two,' he observed, whimsically.

'Ah well, the workmen can get on now,' said the Professor. 'Allow me to congratulate you, my dear colleague, on a masterly piece of work.'

Together they walked back to the ship, where Vargo was waiting, and from where he had watched the end of the Terror. But there was such an unusual expression on his face that the others looked at him enquiringly.

'What's wrong?' asked the Professor. 'Has something happened to upset you?'

'I have news that you will find hard to believe,' answered Vargo, dispassionately.

'What is it? Out with it, my dear chap.'

'Rolto is on Earth.'

Everyone stared.

'On *Earth*!' ejaculated the Professor.

'Impossible,' muttered Tiger.

'It is not impossible. It is true,' said Vargo simply. 'I have been talking to some of his crew. They did not want to speak, but I forced the truth from them. Rolto, dressed like a man of Earth, was landed at a place where later the ship was to pick him up.'

'But what was his idea?' cried the Professor.

'He described his exploit as a scouting expedition.'

'For what purpose?'

'I don't know. He did not say.'

'Now we know who took my suit,' put in Tiger.

'And my books,' said the Professor.

'It also explains why Rolto, when we were on Mino, was so anxious to learn English,' contributed Rex. 'I thought it was queer at the time. I can't think why I didn't suspect the reason.'

'Dear – dear! This is an extraordinary business,' said the

Professor, slowly. 'Still, I can't see that the silly fellow can do any harm. What exactly is the position now, Vargo?'

'The position is this,' stated Vargo. 'When the crew took Rolto's ship back to Earth to pick him up he was not at the appointed place. It has been back twice since, always landing during the hours of darkness of course, but Rolto was not there. When we landed here the crew were about to return to Mino to take the instructions of the High Council.'

'Do you know where Rolto was landed?' asked the Professor. 'Earth is a big place.'

'The crew do not know the name of the region, but they can find it. They describe it as a large open space, purple in colour, with many hills. There is water on both sides of the country.'

'That sounds like Scotland,' observed Tiger.

'I have an idea it is the very place where we landed to pick you up,' announced Vargo.

'Have you a reason for that idea?'

'Yes. Rolto's crew have admitted to me that we were watched on that occasion. Rolto would note the exact spot and suppose it to be safe. For that reason he would choose it for his own landing.'

'Yes, I agree,' murmured the Professor.

'The fellow must be crazy,' declared Toby.

'I don't know. Is he any crazier than us, visiting *his* home town?' The Professor chuckled. 'Perhaps we are all crazy.' He became serious. 'I think we had better push on home right away to see what mischief master Rolto has been into. He always had a bee in his bonnet about Earth. Perhaps by now he has a whole swarm. I imagine there would be no difficulty in our taking Rolto's navigator with us, Vargo, to show us the exact place where he landed his Captain?'

'No difficulty.'

'Then let us go. We shall not need Rolto's ship. If we find him you can bring him home.'

'Very well.'

Toby shook his head. 'With ships coming and going no wonder our newspapers are full of stories of Flying Saucers.'

'By the time we've finished there's likely to be even more talk about them,' observed Rex moodily.

16 The final problem

Within an hour the *Tavona* was on its way to Earth, carrying Rolto's navigator in addition to its normal complement.

A plan put forward by the Professor had been adopted. It was simply this. Rolto's navigator would show them where his captain had been put down. They would then go on to Glensalich Castle for a rest and start their inquiries from there. The landing would be made at night in the hope of avoiding observation. Borron, having unloaded his passengers would not wait, but get out of sight before daybreak. He would return every second night, at midnight by Earthly time, to see if there was any news of Rolto.

Vargo was emphatic that Rolto should not be allowed to remain on Earth even if he wished to do so. The consequences of what he had already done might be serious.

The Professor agreed. 'With all this talk of war and hydrogen bombs going on the people would only have to be told that a Martian had landed to complete the confusion,' he asserted bitterly. 'Even now they don't know what to believe, and would find it hard to recognize the truth if they saw it.'

'Just as well, perhaps,' breathed Toby.

To see his own familiar globe again was to Rex one of the most unreal of his experiences. He was half afraid it would not be in its usual place, and was more than a little relieved to find that it was, with the well-known continental outlines where they should be.

Rolto's navigator, standing beside Borron, guided him down just as the sun was sinking into a haze that hung over the Atlantic Ocean. The shades of night were already falling over Northern Europe and the British Isles.

It was soon clear that the ship was bound for Scotland. Thinking about this as he gazed down at the Moray Firth from his window it occurred to Rex that with land and water so clearly defined from a great altitude there was nothing surprising about the navigator finding his way back to any particular spot. They went on down, the land appearing to float up towards them until, at the finish, so well had Rolto done his spying, the landing was made – as Vargo had forecast – on the hill beside Glensalich.

It would not be easy to describe Rex's sensations as he found his feet once more firmly planted on his own world. It *felt* like home, due no doubt to the conditions in which he had been born – atmospheric pressure, weight, smell and the same old man-in-the-moon looking down from above.

The baggage and equipment were soon unloaded and piled in the heather. Vargo asked if the crew could help to carry it to the house.

The Professor said no. He thought it would be better if the ship didn't tarry in case some prowling poacher or reporter came along.

'My house has been under observation for some time,' he said. 'It would be more prudent not to wait. Remember the arrangement. Midnight every second day, but keep clear if you see red lights. We won't say goodbye as we shall be meeting again so soon.'

Vargo went back into the ship. The doors were closed. The Professor, Tiger, Toby and Rex, stood silent as with only a faint hiss it shot into the clear night sky, soon to be lost to sight. Then, as if the moment did not call for words they walked in silence down the hill into the corrie, each busy with his own thoughts.

Judkins' ultra imperturbability nearly broke down when

he let them in, for as he told them presently, he never expected to see them again.

'Is everything all right?' asked the Professor.

'Yes, sir. There has been no trouble at all. One or two reporters have called, and a man from Scotland Yard with a representative from the Air Ministry; but I told them you were away on holiday, which I think you will agree was no less than the truth, and they took their departure satisfied that no funny business – as it pleased them to call it – was going on. I'll run your baths and prepare some food.'

Judkins had turned away, but came back as if he had remembered something. Unfolding a newspaper flat on the table, and pointing to a picture, he went on: 'I suppose you wouldn't know anything about this, sir?'

An attentive silence fell as the others found themselves staring at a portrait of Rolto.

It was broken by the Professor. 'What – what is all this about, Judkins?' he stammered, in a voice which Rex hardly recognized.

Judkins stared back at them, obviously having had no idea of the effect his question was to have. 'Well, sir,' he explained, 'it seems that this man was arrested as a suspicious character loitering with intent to commit a felony. According to the paper he was taken to Inverness where he told the Chief Constable that he was looking for food. As he spoke with a strange accent he was asked where he had come from and if he had a passport. He said he knew nothing of passports, and at first refused to give any account of himself, but later claimed that he had come from Mars. That was why I mentioned the matter to you, sir.'

'Go on, Judkins. Where is this man now?'

'The paper says that when he insisted that he had come from Mars he was sent to prison for contempt of court.'

'Great heaven!'

'I gather the police are making inquiries about him, and it was for that reason his photograph was published. There is a suspicion that he may be an enemy spy.'

Rex, who had been reading the paragraph in the paper, concluded the story. 'The Inverness police want any person able to identify this man to communicate with them.'

'The wretched fellow is telling the truth,' the Professor informed Judkins. 'He may have come here from Mars but his actual home is much farther away. He is Rolto, the Minoan spaceship captain who abducted the Group-Captain when we were on Mars – and later tried to drive our ship into Jupiter. You will remember the incident.'

'I do indeed, sir.'

'I don't think you ever saw the man close at hand.'

'No, sir. If I remember rightly he had an ambitious project for taking control of Earth.'

'Exactly, and it seems that he has not abandoned it. We met his crew on Mars on our homeward journey. They told us he had been landed on Earth so our intention was to find him. It now seems that the police have found him for us. So much the better. It will save us a lot of trouble. As soon as we have had some refreshment and a rest we will go to Inverness and secure his release – if the police will let him go. Dear – dear. What strange goings on, to be sure.'

'If we tell the Sheriff that what Rolto says is true we're likely to be popped in jail ourselves,' averred Tiger, soberly.

'I'm not proposing to do anything of the sort,' retorted the Professor curtly. 'I only hope this folly of Rolto's doesn't lead to the exposure of our own activities. That would certainly lead to our being put under restraint; and rightly so, for the effect on the community at large might well be devastating. But let us have a meal and get some sleep. In the morning we will start for Inverness.'

It was three o'clock the following afternoon when, in a

hired car, they reached the capital of the Highlands. They went straight to the Chief Constable, in whose office the Professor acted as spokesman.

'I see in the newspaper, sir, that you are anxious to have information about a man giving the name of Rolto,' he began, after having introduced himself and the party.

The officer confirmed that this was correct. 'Can you help us?' he inquired.

'I can indeed,' declared the Professor. 'May I ask where he is now?'

'If he hasn't gone already he'll be going to the lunatic asylum.'

The Professor nearly dropped his spectacles.

'The police doctors have certified him,' went on the Chief, smiling tolerantly. 'All he can talk about is a lot of wild nonsense that he lives on a star and that he came straight here from Mars.'

The Professor sighed, shaking his head sadly. 'Poor fellow. That is what he believes, and while he is humoured he is quite harmless. I have an establishment at Glensalich Castle for those unfortunate people who, while not dangerously insane, suffer from hallucinations. This man who calls himself Rolto is convinced that he is a Martian and talks always of returning to that planet.'

The Chief's eyebrows went up. 'Glensalich? Isn't that the place where people have claimed to have seen these so-called Flying Saucers?'

The Professor nodded. 'Now you have seen one of my patients you will understand why.'

The Chief laughed. 'It explains a lot. I always did take these Flying Saucer yarns with a pinch of salt. If I know anything, your patient will have to wait a long time for a spaceship to take him home.'

'We won't hurt his feelings by telling him that,' said the

Professor, sympathetically. 'As you may imagine, he eluded his guards and made off. If you will return him to my care I will accept responsibility for him and give you an undertaking that he won't worry you any more.'

'Certainly you may take him,' agreed the Chief. 'I shall be glad to be rid of him, for to tell the truth I wasn't quite sure that we'd done the right thing. Nor were the doctors, because in some respects the man not only appeared sane but showed a remarkable degree of intelligence.'

'People who are not quite right in the head are often like that,' returned the Professor casually, as the Chief pressed a bell and gave orders for Rolto to be brought.

When he came into the room, looking tired and worried, Rolto's behaviour should have convinced the police officer that all the Professor had said was true. With a cry of joy, or relief, he ran over and took the Professor's hand. 'Your people are barbarians!' he exclaimed. 'They locked me up. They said I was a criminal. What is a criminal? I have never heard of such a man. We have none in Mino.'

'There – there,' said the Professor kindly. 'Poor fellow. I'm afraid you've had a bad time. Let this be a lesson to you and never run away again.'

'I will stay on Mars,' declared Rolto. 'The people here are all mad. They said I was a liar. What is a liar?'

'A liar,' replied the Professor, 'is a man who does not tell the truth.'

'But I told the truth.'

'Of course you did.'

'Why should a man not tell the truth? Are there people on Earth who do not tell the truth?'

'Quite a lot.'

Rolto looked shocked. 'How terrible. Now I understand some of the things I have seen.'

'So do I,' put in Tiger. 'I see you are wearing my other suit.'

'It was only for a little while, and you weren't using it,' was Rolto's excuse.

'We can talk about that when we get home,' said the Professor kindly.

'Home! So you will take me back to Mars?'

'Of course. The ship is waiting. Come along.' The Professor and the Chief exchanged winks.

One more ordeal awaited Rolto, and that was the car journey to Glensalich; for the man who could flash through space at velocities that defied the imagination was terrified by what he thought were near-collisions on the road. However, the castle was reached safely, and there, while they were waiting for Borron to bring his ship to the rendezvous, he regaled them, often to their amusement, with the story of his adventures on Earth. It was clear that these were just as frightening to him as were those his listeners had experienced among the planetoids. It was equally clear that Rolto had seen all he wanted to of Earth. He could not get away from the awful place fast enough. It was beyond his belief that anyone would wish to stay there.

And so it came about that when, in due course, as arranged, Borron brought his ship to Earth, Rolto Mino, the first man from Space who aspired to explore Earth, lost no time in going aboard.

The last farewell said, the *Tavona* sped away on its timeless, weightless course for home, leaving the Professor and his friends, strangely subdued, to make their way down the hill to the things they knew and understood.

Captain W. E. Johns
Kings of Space 75p

A strange encounter with an amazing scientist named Professor Brane ends with 'Tiger' Clinton and his young son Rex becoming part of the first group of humans to penetrate the unknown vastness beyond this planet Earth.

Their first journeys take them to the desolation of the Moon, the swamps of Venus, and then to the dying world of Mars, where an alien race struggles for life . . .

Return to Mars 75p

'He is taking you within the gravity of Jupiter. There he will leave you, to go on, helpless, into the fires that will burn your ship to a grain of dust . . .'

'Tiger' and his son Rex Clinton travel back to Mars in Professor Brane's spaceship Spacemaster. They meet and befriend some of the ancient and powerful race of Martians, and aid them in their desperate battle to bring life back to a dying world.

To Outer Space 75p

'I have a notion we're going to be the first people from Earth to witness a spaceship dogfight . . .'

By accident, Professor Brane, 'Tiger' Clinton and his young son Rex find their Spacemaster straying into the midst of a cruel interplanetary war which threatens to spread death and destruction through the expanses of outer space.

Nat Hentoff
This School is Driving Me Crazy 70p

Scatty Sam has problems – how can he get on at school when the teachers expect him to be a 'whizz-kid' just because his father's the headmaster! In his efforts to survive the rough and sometimes violent school, Sam ends up having to oppose his father and face expulsion. He knows a gang of bully-boys are threatening the younger kids ... but will he tell on them?

Farley Mowat
The Black Joke 75p

The *Black Joke* is a boat. Everyone knows it's the speediest and nimblest little craft on the coast of Newfoundland. Jonathan Spence is owner and master, and he's got young Peter and Kye as his crew. But a cargo of bootleg liquor and an unwelcome stranger spark off a voyage that sails hard towards danger ...

Lesley Chase
Jill Graham and the Secret of the Silent Pool 75p

Stumbling upon a broken-down shed on the edge of a sinister woodland pool, Jill Graham uncovers an evil plot involving hundreds of pounds, a mysterious red-bearded stranger ... and murder. What is the link between a midnight rendezvous, an underground tunnel and an eccentric old man? And who is it that wants a harmless old man dead?

Michael Hardcastle
Goal 70p

A lot of teenage lads dream of becoming a soccer superstar with a big
name club. A lot of teenage lads just like Barry Dillon . . . but for Barry
it's different. Coming through the school teams he suddenly finds
himself all set to play for Scorton Rovers against some of the biggest
names in soccer . . .

Michael Hardcastle's stories are not just exciting sports fiction for
young readers — they're packed with soccer know-how and technical
tips that make them perfect reading for the young football fan.

Soccer Comes First 75p

Andy Blair, former star of the England squad, is making his comeback
in the game when he becomes captain of Scorton Rovers. He's just
the man to raise the fans' enthusiasm and recapture some of Rovers'
old glory.

With Andy in charge things look great, until Andy's son Bobbie,
Rovers' striker, tangles with the crooks who want to fix matches . . .

You can buy these and other Piccolo books from booksellers and
newsagents ; or direct from the following address :
Pan Books, Sales Office, Cavaye Place, London SW10 9PG
Send purchase price plus 20p for the first book and 10p for
each additional book, to allow for postage and packing,
Prices quoted are applicable in the UK

While every effort is made to keep prices low, it is sometimes
necessary to increase prices at short notice. Pan Books reserve
the right to show on covers and charge new retail prices which
may differ from those advertised in the text or elsewhere